Henry Cuyler Bunner

Love in Old Cloathes and Other Stories

Henry Cuyler Bunner

Love in Old Cloathes and Other Stories

ISBN/EAN: 9783743441842

Manufactured in Europe, USA, Canada, Australia, Japa

Cover: Foto ©Andreas Hilbeck / pixelio.de

Manufactured and distributed by brebook publishing software (www.brebook.com)

Henry Cuyler Bunner

Love in Old Cloathes and Other Stories

Love in Old Cloathes

And Other Stories

"I'M TOMMY BIGGS, MISS LUCRETIA"

Love in Old Cloathes and Other Stories. By H. C. Bunner ✕✕✕✕✕✕✕✕

Illustrated by W. T. Smedley, Orson Lowell, and André Castaigne

Charles Scribner's Sons
New York ∼∼∼∼ 1897

TO

A. L. B.

CONTENTS

LIST OF ILLUSTRATIONS

LOVE IN OLD CLOATHES

LOVE IN OLD CLOATHES

Newe York, yᵉ 1ˢᵗ Aprile, 1883.

Yᴱ worste of my ailment is this, yᵗ it grow-
eth not Less with much nursinge, but is
like to those fevres wᶜʰ yᵉ leeches Starve, 'tis
saide, for that yᵉ more Bloode there be in
yᵉ Sicke man's Bodie, yᵉ more foode is there
for yᵉ Distemper to feede upon.—And it is
moste fittinge yᵗ I come backe to yˢ my
Journall (wherein I have not writt a Lyne
these manye months) on yᵉ 1ˢᵗ of Aprile,
beinge in some Sort myne owne foole and
yᵉ foole of Love, and a poore Butt on whome
his hearte hath play'd a Sorry tricke.—

For it is surelie a strange happenninge,
that I, who am ofte accompted a man of
yᵉ Worlde, (as yᵉ Phrase goes,) sholde be soe
Overtaken and caste downe lyke a Schoole-
boy or a countrie Bumpkin, by a meere
Mayde, & sholde set to Groaninge and
Sighinge, &, for that She will not have me

Sighe to Her, to Groaninge and Sighinge on paper, wch is ye greter Foolishnesse in Me, y^t some one maye reade it Here-after, who hath taken his dose of ye same Physicke, and made no Wrye faces over it; in wch case I doubte I shall be much laugh'd at.—Yet soe much am I a foole, and soe enamour'd of my Foolishnesse, y^t I have a sorte of Shamefull Joye in tellinge, even to my Journall, y^t I am mightie deepe in Love withe ye yonge Daughter of Mistresse Ffrench, and all maye knowe what an Angell is ye Daughter, since I have chose M^rs. French for my Mother in Lawe.—(Though she will have none of my choosinge.)—and I likewise take comforte in ye Fancie, y^t this poore Sheete, wh^on I write, may be made of ye Raggs of some lucklesse Lover, and maye ye more readilie drinke up my complaininge Inke.—

This muche I have learnt y^t Fraunce distilles not, nor ye Indies growe not, ye Remedie for my Aile.—For when I 1st became sensible of ye folly of my Suite, I tooke to drynkinge & smoakinge, thinkinge to cure my minde, but all I got was a head ache, for fellowe to my Hearte ache.—A sorrie Payre! —I then made Shifte, for a while, withe a

Bicycle, but breakinge of Bones mendes no breakinge of Heartes, and 60 myles a Daye bringes me no nearer to a Weddinge.—This being Lowe Sondaye, (wch my Hearte telleth me better than ye Allmanack,) I will goe to Churche ; wh. I maye chaunce to see her.—Laste weeke, her Eastre bonnett vastlie pleas'd me, beinge most cunninglie devys'd in ye mode of oure Grandmothers, and verie lyke to a coales Scuttle, of white satine.—

2nd Aprile.

I trust I make no more moane, than is just for a man in my case, but there is small comforte in lookinge at ye backe of a white Satine bonnett for two Houres, and I maye saye as much.—Neither any cheere in Her goinge out of ye Churche, & Walkinge downe ye Avenue, with a Puppe by ye name of Williamson.

4th Aprile.

Because a man have a Hatt with a Brimme to it like ye Poope-Decke of a Steam-Shippe, and breeches lyke ye Case of an umbrella, and have loste money on Hindoo, he is not therefore in ye beste Societie.—I made this observation, at ye Clubbe, last nighte, in

yͤ hearinge of Wᵐˢᵒⁿ, who made a mightie
Pretence to reade yͤ Spᵗ of yͤ Tymes.—I
doubte it was scurvie of me, but it did me
mucho goode.

7ᵗʰ Aprile.

Yͤ manner of my meetinge with Her and
fallinge in Love with Her (for yͤ two were of
one date) is thus.—I was made acquainte
withe Her on a Wednesdaie, at yͤ House of
Mistresse Varick, ('twas a Reception,) but
did not hear Her Name, nor She myne, by
reason of yͤ noise, and of Mʳˢˢᵉ Varick having
but lately a newe sett of Teethe, of wh. she
had not yet gott, as it were, yͤ just Pitche
and accordance. — I sayde to Her that
yͤ Weather was warm for that season of
yͤ yeare.—She made answer She thought I
was right, for Mʳ Williamson had saide
yͤ same thinge to Her not a minute past.—I
tolde Her She muste not holde it originall or
an Invention of Wᵐˢᵒⁿ, for yͤ Speache had
beene manie yeares in my Familie.—Answer
was made, She wolde be muche bounden to
me if I wolde maintaine yͤ Rightes of my
Familie, and lett all others from usinge of
my propertie, when perceivinge Her to be of

a livelie Witt, I went about to ingage her in
converse, if onlie so I mightie looke into Her
Eyes, wh. were of a coloure suche as I have
never seene before, more like to a Pansie, or
some such flower, than anything else I can
compair with them.—Shortlie we grew most
friendlie, so that She did aske me if I colde
keepe a Secrett.—I answering I colde, She
saide She was anhungered, having Shopp'd
all ye forenoone since Breakfast.—She pray'd
me to gett Her some Foode.—What, I ask'd.
—She answer'd merrilie, a Beafesteake.—I
tolde Her y^t that *Confection* was not on
ye Side-Boarde ; but I presentlie brought
Her such as there was, & She beinge behinde
a Screane, I stoode in ye waie, so y^t none
mighte see Her, & She did eate and drynke
as followeth, to witt —

> iij cupps of Bouillon (wch is a Tea, or Tis-
> ane, of Beafe, made verie hott &
> thinne)
> iv Alberte biscuit
> ij éclairs
> i creame-cake

together with divers small cates and comfeits
wh^of I know not ye names.

So y^t I was grievously afeared for Her Digestion, leste it be over-tax'd. Saide this to Her, however addinge it was my Conceite, y^t by some Processe, lyke Alchemie, wh^{by} ye baser metals are transmuted into golde, so ye grosse mortall foode was on Her lippes chang'd to ye fabled Nectar & Ambrosia of ye Gods.—She tolde me 't was a sillie Speache, yet seam'd not ill-pleas'd withall.— She hath a verie prettie Fashion, or Tricke, of smilinge, when She hath made an end of speakinge, and layinge Her finger upon Her nether Lippe, like as She wolde bid it be stille.—After some more Talke, wh^{in} She show'd that Her Witt was more deepe, and Her minde more seriouslie inclin'd, than I had Thoughte from our first Jestinge, She beinge call'd to go thence, I did see Her mother, whose face I knewe, & was made sensible, y^t I had given my Hearte to ye daughter of a House wh. with myne owne had longe been at grievous Feud, for ye folly of oure Auncestres.—Havinge come to wh. heavie momente in my Tale, I have no Patience to write more to-nighte.

22nd Aprile.

I was mynded to write no more in y^s jour-nall, for verie Shame's sake, y^t I shoude so complayne, lyke a Childe, whose toie is taken f^m him, butt (mayhapp for it is nowe ye fulle Moone, & a moste greavous period for them y^t are Love-strucke) I am fayne, lyke ye Drunkarde who maye not abstayne f^m his cupp, to sett me anewe to recordinge of My Dolorous mishapp.—When I sawe Her agayn, She beinge aware of my name, & of ye divis-ion betwixt oure Houses, wolde have none of me, butt I wolde not be putt Off, & made bolde to question Her, why She sholde me suche exceed^g Coldness.—She answer'd 't was wel knowne what Wronge my Grandefather had done Her G.father.—I saide, She con-founded me with My G.father—we were nott ye same Persone, he beinge muche my Elder, & besydes Dead.—She w^d have it, 't was no matter for jestinge.—I tolde Her I wolde be resolv'd, what grete Wronge y^{is} was.—Y^e more for to make Speache thⁿ for mine owne advertisem^t, for I knewe wel y^e whole Knav-erie, wh. She rehears'd, Howe my G.father had cheated Her G.father of Landes upp y^e River, with more, howe my G.father had im-

pounded y\ :superscript:e Cattle of Hern.—I made answer,
't was foolishnesse, in my mynde, for y\ :superscript:e iii\ :superscript:d
Generation to so quarrell over a Parsel of
rascallie Landes, y\ :superscript:t had long ago beene solde
for Taxes, y\ :superscript:t as to y\ :superscript:e Cowes, I wolde make
them goode, & th\ :superscript:r Produce & Offspringe, if it
tooke y\ :superscript:e whole Wash\ :superscript:tn Markett.—She however tolde me y\ :superscript:t y\ :superscript:e Ffrenche family had
y\ :superscript:e where w\ :superscript:al to buye what they lack'd in
Butter, Beafe & Milke, and likewise in *Veale*,
wh. laste I tooke muche to Hearte, wh. She
seeinge, became more gracious &, on my
pleadinge, accorded y\ :superscript:t I sholde have y\ :superscript:e Priv-
ilege to speake with Her when we next met.
—Butt neyther then, nor at any other tyme
th\ :superscript:after wolde She suffer me to visitt Her. So
I was harde putt to it to compass waies
of gettinge to see Her at such Houses as She
mighte be att, for Routs or Feasts, or y\ :superscript:e
lyke.—

But though I sawe Her manie tymes, oure
converse was ever of y\ :superscript:is Complex\ :superscript:n, & y\ :superscript:e accursed G.father satt downe, and rose upp
with us.—Yet colde I see by Her aspecte, y\ :superscript:t
I had in some sorte Her favoure, & y\ :superscript:t I mis-
lyk'd Her not so gretelie as She w\ :superscript:d have me
thinke.—So y\ :superscript:t one daie, ('t was in Januarie,

& verie colde,) I, beinge moste distrackt, saide to Her, I had tho't 'twolde pleasure Her more, to be friends w. a man, who had a knave for a G.father, y^n with One who had no G.father att alle, lyke W^{mson} (y^e Puppe).— She made answer, I was exceedinge fresshe, or some such matter. She cloath'd her thoughte in phrase more befittinge a Gentlewoman.— Att this I colde no longer contayne myself, but tolde Her roundlie, I lov'd Her, & 't was my Love made me soe unmannerlie.— And w. y^{is} speache I att ye leaste made an End of my Uncertantie, for She bade me speake w. Her no more.—I wolde be determin'd, whether I was Naught to Her.—She made Answer She colde not justlie say I was Naught, seeing y^t wh^{ever} She mighte bee, I was One too manie.—I saide, 't was some Comforte, I had even a Place in Her thoughtes, were it onlie in Her disfavour.—She saide, my Solace was indeede grete, if it kept pace with ye measure of Her Disfavour, for, in plain Terms, She hated me, & on her intreatinge of me to goe, I went.—Y^{is} happ'd att ye house of M^{rss} Varicke, wh. I I^{st} met Her, who (M^{rss} Varicke) was for staying me, y^t I might eate some Ic'd Cream, butt of a Truth I was chill'd to my Taste allreadie.—Albeit I afterwards tooke to walkinge of y⁰ Streets till near Midnight.—'Twas as I saide before in Januarie & exceedinge colde.

20ᵗʰ Maie.

How wearie is yⁱˢ dulle procession of y⁰ Yeare! For it irketh my Soule yᵗ each Monthe shoude come so aptlie after y⁰ Month afore, & Nature looke so Smug, as She had done some grete thinge.—Surelie if she make no Change, she hath work'd no Miracle, for we knowe wel, what we maye look for.— Y⁰ Vine under my Window hath broughte forth Purple Blossoms, as itt hath eache Springe these xii Yeares.—I wolde have had them Redd, or Blue, or I knowe not what Coloure, for I am sicke of likinge of Purple a Dozen Springes in Order.—And wh. moste galls me is yⁱˢ, I knowe howe yⁱˢ sadd Rounde will goe on, & Maie give Place to June, & she to July, & onlie my Hearte blossom not nor my Love growe no greener.

2ⁿᵈ June.

I and my Foolishnesse, we laye Awake last night till y⁰ Sunrise gun, wh. was Shott att 4½ o'ck, & wh. beinge hearde in yᵗ stillnesse fm. an Incredible Distance, seem'd lyke as 'twere a Full Stopp, or Period putt to y^{is} Wakinge-Dreminge, wh^{at} I did turne a newe Leafe in my Counsells, and after much Meditation, have commenc't a newe Chapter, wh. I hope maye leade to a better Conclusion, than them y^t came afore.—For I am nowe resolv'd, & havinge begunn wil carry to an Ende, y^t if I maie not over-come my Passion, I maye at ye least over-com ye Melanchollie, & Spleene, borne y^{of}, & beinge a Lover, be none ye lesse a Man.—To wh. Ende I have come to y^{is} Resolution, to depart fm. ye Towne, & to goe to ye Countrie-House of my Frend, Will Winthrop, who has often intreated me, & has instantly urg'd, y^t I sholde make him a Visitt.—And I take much Shame to myselfe, y^t I have not given him y^{is} Satisfaction since he was married, wh. is nowe ii Yeares.—A goode Fellowe, & I minde me a grete Burden to his Frends when he was in Love, in wh. Plight I mockt him, who am nowe, I much feare me, mockt myselfe.

3rd June.

Pack'd my cloathes, beinge Sundaye. Y^e better ye Daie, ye better ye Deede.

4th June.

Goe downe to Babylon to-daye.

5th Junq.

Att Babylon, att yᵉ Cóttage of Will Winthrop, wh. is no Cottage, but a grete House,
Red, w. Verandahs, & builded in yᵉ Fashⁿ of
Her Maiestie Q. Anne.—Found a mighty
Housefull of People.—Will, his Wife, a verie
proper fayre Ladie, who gave me moste
gracious Reception, Mʳˢˢ Smithe, yᵉ ii Gresham
girles (knowne as yᵒ Titteringe Twins), Bob
White, Virginia Kinge & her Mothʳ, Clarence
Winthrop, & yᵉ whole Alexander Family.—
A grete Gatheringe for so earlie in yᵉ Summer.—In yᵉ Afternoone play'd Lawne-Ten-
niss.—Had for Partner one of yᵒ Twinns,
agˢᵗ Clarence Winthrop & yᵉ other Twinn, wh.
by beinge Confus'd, I loste iii games.—Was
voted a Duffer.—Clarence Winthrop moste
unmannerlie merrie.—He call'd me yᵒ Sad-
Ey'd Romeo, & lykewise cut down yᵉ Ham-
mocke whⁱⁿ I laye, allso tied up my Cloathes
wh. we were att Bath.—He sayde, he Chaw'd
them, a moste barbarous worde for a moste
barbarous Use.—Wh. we were Boyes, & he
did yⁱˢ thinge, I was wont to trounce him

Soundlie, but nowe had to contente Myselfe
w. beatinge of him iii games of Billyardes in
yᵉ Evg., & w. daringe of him to putt on yᵉ
Gloves w. me, for Funne, wh. he mighte not
doe, for I coude knocke him colde.

10ᵗʰ June.

Beinge gon to my Roome somewhatt earlie,
for I found myselfe of a peevish humour,
Clarence came to me, and prayᵈ a few minutes' Speache.—Sayde 't was Love made him
so Rude & Boysterous, he was privilie
betroth'd to his Cozen, Angelica Robertes,
she whose Father lives at Islipp, & colde not
containe Himselfe for Joye.—I sayinge, there
was a Breache in yᵉ Familie, he made Answer,
't was true, her Father & His, beinge Cozens,
did hate each other moste heartilie, butt for
him he cared not for that, & for Angelica,
She gave not a Continentall.—But, sayde I,
Your Consideration matters mightie Little,
synce yᵉ Governours will not heare to it.—He
answered 't was for that he came to me, I
must be his allie, for reason of oure olde
Friendˢᵖ. With that I had no Hearte to
heare more, he made so Light of suche a
Division as parted me & my Happinesse,

but tolde him I was his Frend, wolde serve
him when he had Neede of me, & presentlie
seeing my Humour, he made excuse to goo,
& left me to write downe this, sicke in Mynde,
and thinkinge ever of ye Woman who wil not
oute of my Thoughtes for any change of Place,
neither of employe.—For indeede I doo love
Her moste heartilie, so y^t my Wordes cannot saye it, nor will y^{is} Booke containe it.—
So I wil even goe to Sleepe, y^t in my Dreames
perchaunce my Fancie maye do my Hearte
better Service.

12th June.

She is here.—What Spyte is y^{is} of Fate &
ye alter'd gods! That I, who mighte nott
gett to see Her when to See was to Hope,
muste nowe daylie have Her in my Sight,
stucke lyke a fayre Apple under olde Tan-
talus his Nose.—Goinge downe to ye Hotell
to-day, for to gett me some Tobackoe, was
made aware y^t ye Ffrench familie had hyred
one of ye Cottages round-abouts. — 'T is a
goodlie Dwellinge Without—Would I coude
speake with as much Assurance of ye Inn-
syde!

13th June.

Goinge downe to y⁰ Hotell againe To-day
for more Tobackoe, sawe y⁰ accursed name of
W^mson on y⁰ Registre.— Went about to a
neighboringe Farm & satt me downe behynd
y⁰ Barne, for a ½ an Houre.—Frighted y⁰
Horned Cattle w. talkinge to My Selfe.

15th June.

I wil make an Ende to y^is Businesse.—Wil
make no onger Staye here.—Sawe Her to-
day, driven Home fm. y⁰ Beache, about 4½ of
y⁰ After-noone, by W^mson in his Dogge-
Carte, wh. y⁰ Cadde has broughten here.—
Wil betake me to y⁰ Boundlesse Weste—Not
y^t I care aught for y⁰ Boundlesse Weste, butt
y^t I shal doe wel if haplie I leave my Memou-
rie am^g y⁰ Apaches & bringe Home my Scalpe.

16th June.

To Fyre Islande, in Winthrop's Yacht—y⁰
Twinnes w. us, so Titteringe & Choppinge
Laughter, y^t 't was worse y^n a Flocke of Sand-
pipers.—Found a grete Concourse of people
there, Her amonge them, in a Suite of blue,
y^t became Her bravelie.—She swimms lyke
to a Fishe, butt everie Stroke of Her white

2

Arms (of a lovelie Roundnesse) cleft, as 't
were my Hearte, rather y^n ye Water.—She
bow'd to me, on goinge into ye Water, w. muche
Dignitie, & agayn on Cominge out, but y^{is}
Tyme w. lesse Dignitie, by reason of ye Water
in Her Cloathes, & Her Haire in Her Eyes.—

17th June.

Was for goinge awaie To-morrow, but Clarence cominge againe to my Chamber, &
mightilie purswadinge of me, I feare I am
comitted to a verie sillie Undertakinge.—For
I am promis'd to Help him secretlie to wedd
his Cozen.—He wolde take no Deniall, wolde
have it, his Brother car'd Naughte, 't was but
ye Fighte of theyre Fathers, he was bounde
it sholde be done, & 't were best I stoode his
Witnesse, who was wel lyked of bothe y^e
Braunches of ye Family.—So 't was agree'd,
y^t I shal staye Home to-morrowe fm. ye Ex-
pedition to Fyre Islande, feigning a Head-
Ache, (wh. indeede I meante to do, in any
Happ, for I cannot see Her againe,) & shall
meet him at ye little Churche on ye Southe
Roade. — He to drive to Islipp to fetch
Angelica, lykewise her Witnesse, who sholde
be some One of ye Girles, she hadd not yet

made her Choice.—I made y^{is} Condition, it
sholde not be either of ye Twinnes.—No, nor
Bothe, for that matter.—Inquiringe as to y^e
Clergyman, he sayde ye Dominie was allreadie
Squar'd.

NEWE YORK, Y^E BUCKINGHAM HOTELL, 19th June.

I am come to ye laste Entrie I shall ever
putt downe in y^s Booke, and needes must y^t
I putt it downe quicklie, for all hath Happ'd
in so short a Space, y^t my Heade whirles w.
thynkinge of it. Y^e after-noone of Yester-
daye, I set about Counterfeittinge of a Head-
Ache, & so wel did I compasse it, y^t I verilie
thinke one of ye Twinnes was mynded to
Stay Home & nurse me.—All havinge gone
off, & Clarence on his waye to Islipp, I sett
forth for ye Churche, where arriv'd I founde
it emptie, w. ye Door open. — Went in &
writh'd on ye hard Benches a ¼ of an Houre,
when, hearinge a Sounde, I look'd up &
saw standinge in ye Door-waye, Katherine
Ffrench. — She seem'd muche astonished,
saying You Here! or ye lyke.—I made Answer & sayde y^t though my Familie were
greate Sinners, yet had they never been
Excommunicate by ye Churche.—She sayde,

they colde not Putt Out what never was in.
—While I was bethynkinge me wh. I mighte
answer to y^{is}, she went on, sayinge I must ex-
cuse Her, She wolde goe upp in ye Organ-
Lofte.—I enquiring what for? She sayde to
practice on ye Organ. — She turn'd verie
Redd, of a warm Coloure, as She sayde this.
—I ask'd Do you come hither often? She
replyinge Yes, I enquir'd how ye Organ lyked
Her.—She sayde Right well, when I made
question more curiously (for She grew more
Redd eache moment) how was ye Action? y^e
Tone? how manie Stopps? Wh^{at} She grow-
inge gretelie Confus'd, I led Her into y^e
Churche, & show'd Her y^t there was no Or-
gan, y^t Choire beinge indeede a Band, of i
Tuninge-Forke, i Kitt, & i Horse-Fiddle.—At
this She fell to Smilinge & Blushinge att one
Tyme.—She perceiv'd our Errandes were y^e
Same & crav'd Pardon for Her Fibb.—I
tolde Her, If She came Thither to be Wit-
ness at her Frend's Weddinge, 'twas no greate
Fibb, 'twolde indeede be Practice for Her.—
This havinge a rude Sound, I added I thankt
ye Starrs y^t had bro't us Together. She sayde
if ye Starrs appoint'd us to meete no oftener
y^n this Couple shoude be Wedded, She was

wel content. This cominge on me lyke a last
Buffett of Fate, that She shoude so despite-
fully intreat me, I was suddenlie Seized with
so Sorrie a Humour, & withal so angrie, y^t I
colde scarce Containe myselfe, but went &
Sat downe neare ye Doore, lookinge out till
Clarence shd. come w. his Bride.—Looking
over my Sholder, I sawe y^t She wente fm.
Windowe to Windowe within, Pluckinge y^e
Blossoms fm. ye Vines, & settinge them in her
Girdle.—She seem'd most tall and faire, &
swete to look uponn, & itt Anger'd me y^e
More.—Meanwhiles, She discours'd pleasant-
lie, asking me manie questions, to the wh. I
gave but shorte and churlish answers. She
ask'd Did I nott Knowe Angelica Roberts was
Her best Frend? How longe had I knowne
of ye Betrothal? Did I thinke 'twolde knitt
ye House together, & Was it not Sad to see a
Familie thus Divided?—I answer'd Her, I
wd. not robb a Man of ye precious Righte to
Quarrell with his Relations.—And then, with
meditatinge on ye goode Lucke of Clarence,
& my owne harde Case, I had suche a sudden Rage of peevishness y^t I knewe scarcelie
what I did. Soe when she ask'd me merrilie
why I turn'd my Backe on Her, I made

Reply I had turn'd my Backe on much
Follie. — Wh. was no sooner oute of my
Mouthe than I was mightilie Sorrie for it,
and turninge aboute, I perceiv'd She was in
Teares & weepinge bitterlie. Wh^at my Hearte
wolde holde no More, & I rose upp & tooke
Her in my arms & Kiss'd & Comforted Her,
She makinge no Denyal, but seeminge great-
lie to Neede such Solace, wh. I was not
Loathe to give Her.—Whiles we were at
This, onlie She had gott to Smilinge, & to
sayinge of Things which even y^is paper shal
not knowe, came in ye Dominie, sayinge
He judg'd We were the Couple he came
to Wed.—With him ye Sexton & ye Sexton's
Wife. — My swete Kate, alle as rosey as
Venus's Nape, was for Denyinge of y^is, butt I
wolde not have it, & sayde Yes.—She remon-
strating w. me, privilie, I tolde Her She must
not make me Out a Liar, y^t to Deceave y^e
Man of God were a greavous Sinn, y^t I had
gott Her nowe, & wd. not lett her Slipp
from me, & did soe Talke Her Downe, & w.
such Strengthe of joie, y^t allmost before She
knewe it, we Stoode upp, & were Wed, w. a
Ringe (tho' She Knewe it nott) wh. belong'd
to My G father.   (Him y^t Cheated Her^n.)—

Wh was no sooner done, than in came Clarence & Angelica, & were Wedded in theyre Turn.—The Clergyman greatelie surprised, but more att ye Largeness of his Fee.

This Businesse being Ended, we fled by ye Trayne of 4½ o'cke, to y^is Place, where we wait till ye Bloode of all ye Ffrenches have Tyme to coole downe, for ye wise Mann who meeteth his Mother in Lawe ye 1st tyme, wil meete her when she is Milde.—

And so I close y^is Journall, wh., tho' for ye moste Parte 'tis but a peevish Scrawle, hath one Page of Golde, wh^on I have writt ye laste strange Happ wh^by I have layd Williamson by ye Heeles & found me ye sweetest Wife y^t ever

.   .   .

stopp'd a man's Mouthe w. kisses for writinge of Her Prayses.

A LETTER
AND A PARAGRAPH

A LETTER
AND A PARAGRAPH

I

THE LETTER

NEW YORK, NOV. 16, 1883.

MY DEAR WILL :—

You cannot be expected to remember it, but this is the fifth anniversary of my wedding-day, and to-morrow—it will be to-morrow before this letter is closed—is my birthday—my fortieth. My head is full of those thoughts which the habit of my life moves me to put on paper, where I can best express them; and yet which must be written for only the friendliest of eyes. It is not the least of my happiness in this life that I have one friend to whom I can unlock my heart as I can to you.

The wife has just been putting your namesake to sleep. Don't infer that, even on the occasion of this family feast, he has been allowed to sit up until half past eleven. He went to bed properly enough, with a tear or two, at eight ; but when his mother stole into his room just now, after her custom, I heard his small voice raised in drowsy inquiry ; and I followed her, and slipped the curtain of the doorway aside, and looked. But I did not go into the room.

The shaded lamp was making a yellow glory in one spot—the head of the little brass crib where my wife knelt by my boy. I saw the little face, so like hers, turned up to her. There was a smile on it that I knew was a reflection of hers. He was winking in a merry half-attempt to keep awake ; but wakefulness was slipping away from him under the charm of that smile that I could not see. His brown eyes closed, and opened for an instant, and closed again as the tender, happy hush of a child's sleep settled down upon him, and he was gone where we in our heavier slumbers shall hardly follow him. Then, before I could see my wife's face as she bent and kissed him, I let the curtain fall, and crept back here, to sit by the last of the fire, and see that sacred sight again with the spiritual eyes, and to dream wonderingly over the unspeakable happiness that has in some mysterious way come to me, undeserving.

I tell you, Will, that moment was to me like one of those moments of waking that we know in childhood, when we catch the going of a dream too subtly sweet to belong to this earth—a glad vision, gone before our eyes can open wide; not to be figured into any earthly idea, leaving in its passage a joy so high and fine that the poets tell us it is a memory of some heaven from which our young souls are yet fresh.

You can understand how it is that I find it hard to realize that there can be such things in my life; for you know what that life was up to a few years ago. I am like a man who has spent his first thirty years in a cave. It takes more than a decade above ground to make him quite believe in the sun and the blue of the sky.

I was sitting just now before the hearth, with my feet in the bearskin rug you sent us two Christmases ago. The light of the low wood fire was chasing the shadows around

the room, over my books and my pictures,
and all the fine and gracious luxuries with
which I may now make my eyes and my
heart glad, and pamper the tastes that grow
with feeding. I was taking count, so to
speak, of my prosperity—the material treasures, the better treasure that I find in such
portion of fame as the world has allotted me,
and the treasure of treasures across the thresh-
old of the next room—in the next room?   No
—there, here, in every room, in every corner
of the house, filling it with peace, is the gentle and holy spirit of love.

As I sat and thought, my mind went back
to the day that you and I first met, twenty-
two years ago—twenty-two in February next.
In twenty-two years more I could not forget
that hideous first day in the city room of the
Morning Record.   I can see the great gloomy
room, with its meagre gas-jets lighting up,
here and there, a pale face at a desk, and
bringing out in ghastly spots the ugliness of
the ink-smeared walls.   A winter rain was
pouring down outside.   I could feel its chill
and damp in the room, though little of it was
to be seen through the grimy window-panes.
The composing-room in the rear sent a smell

of ink and benzine to permeate the moist atmosphere. The rumble and shiver of the great presses printing the weekly came up from below. I sat there in my wet clothes and waited for my first assignment. I was eighteen, poor as a church mouse, green, desperately hopeful after a boy's fashion, and with nothing in my head but the Latin and Greek of my one single year at college. My spirit had sunk down far out of sight. My heart beat nervously at every sound of that awful city editor's voice, as he called up his soldiers one by one and assigned them to duty. I could only silently pray that he would " give me an easy one," and that I should not disgrace myself in the doing of it. By Jove, Will, what an old martinet Baldwin was, for all his good heart ! Do you remember that sharp, crackling voice of his, and the awful " Be brief ! be brief ! " that always drove all capacity for condensation out of a man's head, and set him to stammering out his story with wordy incoherence. Baldwin is on the *Record* still. I wonder what poor devil is trembling at this hour under that disconcerting adjuration.

A wretched day that was ! The hours went slow as grief. Smeary little bare-armed

fiends trotted in from the composing-room
and out again, bearing fluttering galley-
proofs. Bedraggled, hollow-eyed men came
in from the streets and set their soaked umbrellas to steam against the heater, and
passed into the lion's den to feed him with
news, and were sent out again to take up
their half-cooked umbrellas and go forth to
forage for more. Everyone, I thought, gave
me one brief glance of contempt and curi-
osity, and put me out of his thoughts. Everyone had some business—everyone but me.
The men who had been waiting with me were
called up one by one and detailed to work. I
was left alone.

Then a new horror came to torture my nervously active imagination. Had my superior
officer forgotten his new recruit? Or could
he find no task mean enough for my powers?
This filled me at first with a sinking shame,
and then with a hot rage and sense of wrong.
Why should he thus slight me? Had I not
a right to be tried, at least? Was there any
duty he could find that I would not perform
or die? I would go to him and tell him that
I had come there to work; and would make
him give me the work. No, I should simply

be snubbed, and sent to my seat like a school-
boy, or perhaps discharged on the spot. I
must bear my humiliation in silence.

I looked up and saw you entering, with
your bright, ruddy boy's face shining with
wet, beaming a greeting to all the room. In
my soul I cursed you, at a venture, for your
lightheartedness and your look of cheery self-
confidence. What a vast stretch of struggle
and success set you above me—you, the re-
porter, above me, the novice! And just then
came the awful summons—"Barclay! Barclay!"—I shall hear that strident note at the
judgment day. I went in and got my orders,
and came out with them, all in a sort of daze
that must have made Baldwin think me an
idiot. And then you came up to me and
scraped acquaintance in a desultory way, to
hide your kind intent; and gave me a hint
or two as to how to obtain a full account of
the biennial meeting of the Post-Pliocene
Mineralogical Society, or whatever it was,
without diving too deeply into the Post-Pliocene period. I would have fought for you
to the death, at that moment.

'Twas a small matter, but the friendship
begun in manly and helpful kindness has
3

gone on for twenty-two years in mutual faith
and loyalty; and the growth dignifies the seed.

A sturdy growth it was in its sapling days.
It was in the late spring that we decided to
take the room together in St. Mark's Place.
A big room and a poor room, indeed, on the
third story of that "battered caravanserai,"
and for twelve long years it held us and our
hopes and our despairs and our troubles and
our joys.

I don't think I have forgotten one detail of
that room. There is the generous old fire-
place, insultingly bricked up by modern poverty, all save the meagre niche that holds our
fire—when we can have a fire. There is the
great second-hand table—our first purchase
—where we sit and work for immortality in
the scant intervals of working for life. Your
drawer, with the manuscript of your "Con-
cordance of Political Economy," is to the
right. Mine is to the left; it holds the unfinished play, and the poems that might better have been unfinished. There are the two
narrow cots—yours to the left of the door as
you enter; mine to the right.

How strange that I can see it all so clearly, now that all is different!

Yet I can remember myself coming home at one o'clock at night, dragging my tired feet up those dark, still, tortuous stairs, gripping the shaky baluster for aid. I open the door —I can feel the little old-fashioned brass knob in my palm even now—and I look to the left. Ah, you are already at home and in bed. I need not look toward the table. There is money—a little—in the common treasury; and, in accordance with our regular compact, I know there stand on that table twin bottles of beer, half a loaf of rye bread, and a double palm's-breadth of Swiss cheese. You are staying your hunger in sleep; for one may not eat until the other comes. I will wake you up, and we shall feast together and talk over the day that is dead and the day that is begun.

Strange, is it not, that I should have some trouble to realize that this is only a memory, —I, with my feet in the bearskin rug that it would have beggared the two of us, or a dozen like us, to purchase in those days. Strange that my mind should be wandering on the crude work of my boyhood and my early manhood. I who have won name and fame, as the world would say. I, to whom

young men come for advice and encourage-
ment, as to a tried veteran! Strange that I
should be thinking of a time when even your
true and tireless friendship could not quench
a subtle hunger at my heart, a hunger for a
more dear and intimate comradeship. I, with
the tenderest of wives scarce out of my sight;
even in her sleep she is no further from me
than my own soul.

Strangest of all this, that the mad agony of
grief, the passion of desolation that came
upon me when our long partnership was dis-
solved for ever, should now be nothing but a
memory, like other memories, to be sum-
moned up out of the resting-places of the
mind, toyed with, idly questioned, and dismissed with a sigh and a smile! What a
real thing it was just ten years ago; what a
very present pain! Believe me, Will,—yes,
I want you to believe this—that in those first
hours of loneliness I could have welcomed
death; death would have fallen upon me as
calmly as sleep has fallen upon my boy in
the room beyond there.

You knew nothing of this then; I suppose
you but half believe it now; for our parting
was manly enough. I kept as stiff an upper

lip as you did, for all there was less hair on it. Perhaps it seems extravagant to you. But there was a deal of difference between our cases. You had turned your pen to money-making, at the call of love; you were going to Stillwater to marry the judge's daughter, and to become a great land-owner and mayor of Stillwater and millionnaire—or what is it now? And much of this you foresaw or hoped for, at least. Hope is something. But for me? I was left in the third-story of a poor lodging-house in St. Mark's Place, my best friend gone from me; with neither remembrance nor hope of Love to live on, and with my last story back from *all* the magazines.

We will not talk about it. Let me get back to my pleasant library with the books and the pictures and the glancing fire-light, and me with my feet in your bearskin rug, listening to my wife's step in the next room.

To your ear, for our communion has been so long and so close that to either one of us the faintest inflection of the other's voice speaks clearer than formulated words; to your ear there must be something akin to a tone of regret—regret for the old days—in

what I have just said. And would it be
strange if there were? A poor soldier of
fortune who had been set to a man's work
before he had done with his meagre boyhood,
who had passed from recruit to the place of
a young veteran in that great, hard-fighting,
unresting pioneer army of journalism; was
he the man, all of a sudden, to stretch his
toughened sinews out and let them relax in
the glow of the home hearth? Would not
his legs begin to twitch for the road; would
he not be wild to feel again the rain in his
weather-beaten face? Would you think it
strange if at night he should toss in his white,
soft bed, longing to change it for a blanket
on the turf, with the broad procession of sun-
lit worlds sweeping over his head, beyond
the blue spaces of the night? And even if
the dear face on the pillow next him were to
wake and look at him with reproachful surprise; and even if warm arms drew him back
to his new allegiance; would not his heart in
dreams go throbbing to the rhythm of the
drum or the music of songs sung by the camp-
fire?

It was so at the beginning, in the incredible happiness of the first year, and even after

the boy's birth. Do you know, it was
months before I could accept that boy as a
fact? If, at any moment, he had vanished
from my sight, crib and all, I should not
have been surprised. I was not sure of him
until he began to show his mother's eyes.

Yes, even in those days some of the old
leaven worked in me. I had moments of
that old barbaric freedom which we used to
rejoice in—that feeling of being answerable
to nothing in the world save my own will—
the sense of untrammeled, careless power.

Do you remember the night that we walked
till sunrise? You remember how hot it was
at midnight, when we left the office, and how
the moonlight on the statue above the City
Hall seemed to invite us fieldward, where no
gaslight glared, no torches flickered. So we
walked idly northward, through the black,
silence-stricken down-town streets; through
that feverish, unresting central region that
lies between the vileness of Houston Street
and the calm and spacious dignity of the
brown-stone ways, where the closed and
darkened dwellings looked like huge tombs
in the pallid light of the moon. We passed
the suburban belt of shanties; we passed the

garden-girt villas beyond them, and it was
from the hill above Spuyten Duyvil that we
saw the first color of the morning upon the
face of the Palisades.

It would have taken very little in that moment to set us off to tramping the broad
earth, for the pure joy of free wayfaring.
What was there to hold us back? No tie of
home or kin. All we had in the world to
leave behind us was some futile scribbling on
various sheets of paper. And of that sort of
thing both our heads were full enough. I
think it was but the veriest chance that,
having begun that walk, we did not go on
and get our fill of wandering, and ruin our
lives.

Well, that same wild, adventurous spirit
came upon me now and then. There were
times when, for the moment, I forgot that I
had a wife and a child. There were times
when I remembered them as a burden. Why
should I not say this? It is the history of
every married man,—at least of every manly
man,—though he be married to the best
woman in the world. It means no lack of
love. It is as unavoidable as the leap of the
blood in you that answers a trumpet-call.

At first I was frightened, and fought against it as against something that might grow upon me. I reproached myself for disloyalty in thought. Ah! what need had *I* to fight? What need had I to choke down rebellious fancies, while my wife's love was working that miracle that makes two spirits one?

What is it, this union that comes to us as a surprise, and remains for all outside an incommunicable mystery? What is this that makes our unmarried love seem so slight and childish a thing? You and I, who know it, know that it is no mere fruit of intimacy and usage, although in its growth it keeps pace with these. We know that in some subtle way it has been given to a man to see a woman's soul as he sees his own, and to a woman to look into a man's heart as if it were, indeed, hers. But the friend who sits at my table, seeing that my wife and I understand each other at a simple meeting of the eyes, makes no more of it than he does of the glance of intelligence which, with close friends, often takes the place of speech. He never dreams of the sweet delight with which we commune together in a language that he cannot understand—that he cannot hear—a language that has no formulated words, feeling answering feeling.

It is not wonderful that I should wish to give expression to the gratitude with which I have seen my life made to blossom thus ; my thankfulness for the love which has made me not only a happier, but, I humbly believe, a wiser and a better-minded man. But I know too well the hopelessness of trying to find words to describe what, were I a poet, my best song might but faintly, faintly echo.

I thought I heard a rustle behind me just now. In a little while my wife will come softly into the room, and softly up to where I am sitting, stepping silently across your bearskin rug, and will lay one hand softly on my left shoulder, while the other slips down this arm with which I write, until it falls and closes lightly, yet with loving firmness, on my hand that holds the pen. And I shall say, "Only the last words to Will and his wife, dear." And she will release my hand, and will lift her own, I think, to caress the patch of gray hair on my temple; it is a way she has, as though it were some pitiful scar, and she will say, "Give them my love, and tell them they must not fail us this Christmas. I want them to see how our Willy has grown." And when she says "Our Willy," the hand on my shoulder will instinctively close a little, clingingly; and she will bend her head, and put her face close to mine, and I shall turn to look into her eyes.

. . . . ,

Bear with me, my dear Will, until I have told you why I have written this letter and what it means. I have concealed one thing from you for the last six months. I have disease of the heart, and the doctor has told me that I may die at any moment. Somehow, I think—I know the moment is close at hand; I shall soon go to that narrow cot on the right of the door, and I do not believe I shall wake up in the morning with the sun in my eyes, to look across the room and see that its companion is gone.

For I am in the old room, Will, as you know, and it is not ten years since you went away, but two days. The picture that has seemed real to me as I wrote these pages is fading, and the thin gas-jet flickers and sinks as it always did in these first morning hours.

I can hear the roar of the last Harlem train swell and sink, and the sharp clink of car-bells break the silence that follows. The wind is gasping and struggling in the chimney, and blowing a white powdery ash down on the hearth. I have just burnt my poems and the play. Both the table drawers are empty now ; and soon enough the two empty chairs will stare at each other across the bare table. What a wild dream have I dreamt in all this emptiness ! Just now, I thought indeed that it was true. I thought I heard a woman's step behind me, and I turned—

Peace be with you, Will, in the fulness of your love. I am going to sleep. Perhaps I shall dream it all again, and shall hear that soft footfall when the turn of the night comes, and the pale light through the ragged blind, and the end of a long loneliness.

After I am dead, I wish you to think of me not as I was, but as I wanted to be. I have tried to show you that I have led by your side a happier and dearer life of hope and aspiration than the one you saw. I have tried to leave your memory a picture of me that you will not shrink from calling up when you have a quiet hour and time for thought of the friend whom you knew well ; but whom you may, perhaps, know better now that he is dead.

REGINALD BARCLAY.

II

THE PARAGRAPH

[From the *New York Herald* of Nov. 18, 1883.]

Reginald Barclay, a journalist, was found dead in his bed at 15 St. Mark's Place, yesterday morning. No inquest was held, as Mr. Barclay had been known to be suffering from disease of the heart, and his death was not unexpected. The deceased came originally from Oneida County, and was regarded as a young journalist of considerable promise. He had been for some years on the city staff of the *Record*, and was the correspondent of several out-of-town papers. He had also contributed to the monthly magazines, occasional poems and short stories, which showed the possession, in some measure, of the imaginative faculty. Mr. Barclay was about thirty years of age, and unmarried.

"AS ONE HAVING AUTHORITY "

"AS ONE HAVING AUTHORITY"

THE ramshackle little train of three cars was joggling slowly on as only a Southern railroad train can joggle, its whole frame shaking and jarring and rattling in an agony of exertion, utterly out of proportion to the progress it was making. It put me in mind, somehow, of the way a very aged negro saws wood when he sees charitable gentlefolk coming along the road.

In the seat beside me Mr. John McMarsters fidgeted — fidgeted for New York, for the New York papers, for news of the races, for somebody to talk horse with, for a game of cards, or pool, or billiards, or anything that could be called a game. These were the things that made life sweet to Handsome Jack, and these things being denied him for the time being, he fidgeted. He tugged at his great fair mustaches, shifted about his

4

seat, twisted and untwisted his long legs; his face twitched and grimaced, and from time to time he swore under his breath in a futile and scattering way.

Then his light-blue boyish eyes began to wander over the car in a blank, searching stare, and I knew he was looking for "a real live sport." Yes, I knew he would gladly have exchanged my society for that of the humblest jockey from a Kentucky stable, and that our twenty years of friendship would count as naught in the balance. Yet I did not repine. It is the way of the world. I turned to my book and took a walk with Mr. John Evelyn to see King Charles go by.

Suddenly I felt Jack grasp my arm.

"Say!" he said, "look there! What kind of a boss parson do you call that?"

He pointed to a magnificent old man in the dress of the church, who sat facing us at the other end of the car.

"How's that?" said Jack, who had been graduated of the Bowery and dropped by Columbia College. "Get on to the physique! Why, that man has no business to be a dom-inie. He was built to fight. Say! he must

have been right in his good time when Hee-
nan and Morrissey were on deck. He must
have been a beautiful man. How do you
suppose they ever got him to take a religious
job? "

"John," said I, laying down my book,
"I know that your life is practically circum-
scribed by the race-track, and that you are
a bigoted and intolerant sport. But *will* you
tell me how an old New Yorker like you, and
an old Ninth Warder, can get to your age
without knowing Bishop Waldegrave, by
sight, at least."

"Well," said Jack, flushing a little, "I
suppose he keeps off *my* beat; and I don't
worry *his* very much. But I'll tell you one
thing, my friend. I don't know much about
bishops, but I do know something about
men, and I pick this man out of this car—
see? And I'm going to make his acquaintance."

"What do you mean?" I cried, aghast.

"Mean?" repeated Jack. "I mean I'm
going to introduce myself to him. He looks
as if he'd like to have a little talk with a
white man. Who's that fellow with him—
that sour little prune? "

"That's his nephew, Frederick Dillington," said I.

"Is it?" said Jack. "Well, I bet he's just waiting for the old man's wealth. I'll bet it on his face. Say! what wages does a bishop get? He's got big money, hasn't he? Thought so. Look at that English valet in the seat behind him. That's the correctest thing I ever saw, and the correct thing comes high. Too correct for me. I'm glad *my* man isn't like that. I wouldn't come home to that man at three o'clock in the morning for five hundred dollars. Why, it would be just an act of holy charity to go over and brighten that bishop up a bit. Come along!"

I talked my best to Jack. I tried my best to make him understand who and what Bishop Waldegrave was, or rather had been. I told him that the Bishop had been in his time the greatest man in his Church, and that he was famous the world over for his scholarship, his philanthropy, his vast abilities, and his splendid oratory, and his power over the hearts and minds of men. I told him that he had long ago retired from active life, and that it was more than suspected that his great mind was failing with his advancing years. I tried to explain to the honest soul that our company might not be acceptable to such a man. Then I made a hopeless blunder.

"Why, Jack," I said, "think of his age! That man may have baptized your father, and perhaps mine, for all I know."

"That does it," said Jack, rising promptly. "It's a long shot, but I take the chances. I'm going to ask him." And he sped down the aisle.

Three minutes later, I looked over the top of my Evelyn, and saw the Bishop and Jack holding the friendliest of converse, while Mr. Dillington glared at them in an unpleasant way, and the English valet took the strange scene in without anything in his face that could remotely suggest an expression. It is one peculiar thing about human nature that there is always a great deal to learn about it.

But now I began to feel uneasy on my own account. I felt sure that Jack, in the simple hospitality of his spirit, would take me into his new friendship; and I felt that much might be pardoned to Jack that might not be pardoned to me. I went back into the smoking-car, which was in the rear of the train—it was one of those trains that travel down **the** road with one end foremost, and **up** with the other end in front.

I had smoked two cigars, and was wondering how long I could hold out, when my astonished eyes saw Jack McMarsters appear in the doorway, with the Bishop leaning on his arm.

"All right, now, Bishop," I heard him say, **as he** and his tall charge got safely within the car, "free before the wind!"

With athletic skill, yet with a gentleness that was pretty to see, he guided the old man to the seat which I rose to give him. Then, as we settled ourselves opposite, he presented me to Bishop Waldegrave, in his own easy fashion.

"**I** knew you'd **want** to know the Bishop," he remarked **to** me, airily, after the brief ceremony was over. "He did baptize my father, and he thinks he baptized yours. Can you give him any pointers on your old man?"

I looked at the Bishop. He did not smile. He had accepted Jack just as all Jack's friends had accepted him. The old man's broad charity, and **the** profound knowledge

"'ALL RIGHT NOW, BISHOP,' I HEARD HIM SAY"

of the world which he had possessed in his
days of active service, had opened the way to
his heart for all sorts and conditions of men,
who bore the passport of genuineness. That
passport being undoubtedly in Jack's possession, it made no difference to the Bishop
that he spoke a peculiar dialect of the
English language.

Moreover, we had not talked a quarter of
an hour before I discovered that Jack's inter-
pretation of the expression that the old
man's face had worn was absolutely right.
His kind and happy spirit *was* yearning
for good fellowship. There was that in him
which craved better companionship than
his cold and soulless caretakers could give
him. The dignified, thoughtful lines of
his face softened as he talked to us in
an eager, pleased way, rambling on of old
times and old houses, and the good men
and the dear women whom he had wed and
buried. He seemed to grow younger as he
talked.

But in a very short time he showed that he
was tired, and, lying back in his seat, he fell
into that curious light slumber of old age
that is not all sleep, but is partly a dim

revery. Jack watched him carefully until he
was "off"—as Jack expressed it—and then
he whispered softly to me.

"Great, ain't he? Wish you could have
seen the fun when I started to take him in
here. Nephew tried to make him believe he
didn't want to come. Old man wouldn't have
it. Said he thought a cigar would do him
good. Nephew tried it again—I couldn't
hear what he said. Then the old man got
right up on his choker. His voice was just
as sweet and mild as a May morning, but
when he put the emphatics on, it sounded
like a chunk of ice falling off a five-story
building. 'Fred-er-ick,' says he, 'I am GO-
ING into the SMOKING-CAR to have a
little CONVERSATION with the grandson
of my old FRIEND, Judge McMarsters. I
will see you, Frederick, on my RETURN.'
Frederick turned pale green, and sat down.
He just muttered something about sending
the valet with him in case he wanted anything. I waited until the Bishop had a move
on him, and then I slipped back and tapped
Nephew Fred on the shoulder. 'Look here,'
says I, 'your man stays just where he is.
You may not have had a father yourself, but

I have.' You don't think I said too much,
do you ? "

" Oh, no, not at all," said I, " not in the
least. He would have been quite justified in
throwing you out of the car, that's all."

" That fellow ? " said Jack, disdainfully ;
" why, he couldn't lift one side of me." And
I gave it up.

" Now, you said," continued Jack, nodding
toward the dozing Bishop, " that his head
was going. 'Tisn't, though. It's nothing
but old age. When a man gets to be as old
as that, he talks a while and then he kind of
loses his grip, just for a minute—see ? All
he needs is a little help. My old father was
like that for the last six years of his life, and
I learned how to manage him. When I saw
he was likely to go to pieces, I just put my
hand on him—*so*—quiet, but firm ; and I
whispered to him very low : ' Steady down,
Governor, steady down—don't break ! Then
he pulled himself right together; and if he
thought nobody had noticed him he'd be just
as straight as you or I. That's the way to
handle them ! "

I was wondering if this was the way he
had " handled " Bishop Waldegrave, when the

train began to slow down by a little variation
on the series of jerks and bumps, and the
negro brakeman put his head in the doorway
and shouted :

"Ashe River Ferry!"

The Bishop still dozed—in fact, he was
fast asleep now—too sound asleep to be
awakened by the bump with which we finally
stopped. Jack and I went to the door and
looked out. We saw a forlorn place at the
forlornest hour of a forlorn day. Even in
full summer, Ashe River Ferry could not
have been an attractive town. Seen in the
dim light of a late spring evening, it was a
singularly depressing specimen of the shift-
less and poverty-stricken little settlements
that dot the waste spaces of the South—towns,
if towns they may be called, that come into
existence solely to supply the special needs
of some little group of railroad operatives. A
dozen hideously ugly frame houses, forty or
fifty negro shanties, a few acres of wretched
farm-land, sparsely bristled with dead corn-
stalks, one to a hill ; blackened stumps spot-
ting great stretches of half-cleared land ; thin,
sickly pine-woods hemming in the horizon on
three sides ; on the fourth a broad, muddy,

dreary river, swoollen and turbulent from tho spring freshets, with the same poor pine-woods on the other side, scratches of black against the one pale-yellow line that cleft the dull gray sky to the eastward. If one lived a hundred years at Ashe River Ferry, he could make no more of it than this.

Looking out on this unengaging prospect, I was surprised to see Jack's face suddenly light up with mirth, and to hear him break into a low, happy laugh. Then he touched my shoulder and pointed down the track.

"How's that for a joke on tho nephew?" he said.

I looked down toward the river at tho little ferry-slip, with its crazy piles and rusty chains. The ferry-boat, which was likewise crazy and rusty, could carry but one car at a time, and it had just started on its first trip with car No. 1 of our train. On the rear platform stood two figures—the impassive English valet and Mr. Frederick Dillington, who was anything but impassive. We were too far away to hear what he was saying to the stolid deckhands below him, but there was not the slightest need of words to explain the situation, or to make us understand that Mr. Dillington was executing every variation in his power on the simple theme of "stop the boat!"—and that his solo was receiving choral responses of "it can't be done."

And it was not done. The ferry-boat puffed and wheezed on her way as well as she was able—and, indeed, nothing but the strange stupidity of selfishness could have blinded Mr. Dillington to the fact that, in such wild and rough water, the clumsy craft could ill afford to go one foot further than was absolutely needful.

Jack leaned forward with his hands on his knees, his face fairly wrinkled with merriment, and he crowed and chuckled with glee.

"Oh, I'd have given a hundred dollars for this!" he said. "And if that boat gets stuck on the other side, I make it five hundred."

"John," I said, "is not this one of the occasions when you are an idiot? What should we do if we were left with that old gentleman on our hands?"

"Why," said Jack, heartily and simply, "bless your soul, *I'd* take care of him! I'd give him a better time than he's had in twenty years, too; and don't you make a mistake."

That day, for sure, the gods were with Mr.

John McMarsters. The ferry-boat did not get stuck on the other side, to his deep disappointment, but she fulfilled his desire by a different method of procedure—she fixed things, as he remarked, in her own blooming, pig-headed way.

For, on her return trip, as she approached the shore, she ran well up the river to avoid being carried past her slip by the furious current, and, miscalculating her direction, came against the trembling old spiles with a force that wrecked nearly half one side of the slip, and smashed her own wheel-box into a tangle of kindling wood and twisted iron.

"Great Cæsar's Ghost!" shouted Jack, pounding his knees with delight, "she's done it, she's done it! Say! who do I pay that five hundred to? Do the niggers get it, or do I blow it in on the Bishop?"

I tried to point out some of the serious aspects of the case to Jack, but he would have none of my remonstrances.

"It's an elegant, gilt-edged lark," he said. "I'm game for it, and so are you, when you get through with your preaching. Eloping with a bishop! Holy *Moses!* Wait till I get back to New York and tell the boys!"

"But," said I, "it may be possible to get a boat across the river. I will go and inquire."

The veteran sport withered me with superior scorn.

"You may inquire, if you like," he said, "till your inquirer breaks, but *I* don't want any man to tell me he can get a boat across that river. Why, I wouldn't take a ship's yawl out there. Man, it's half a flood!"

I did inquire, however, and was scorned and despised by every native to whom I addressed my inquiry; so we went back to the car to break the news to the Bishop, who was awake by this time.

At first he took it quite hard. He seemed to be distressed and apprehensive, and said, "Oh, dear, oh, dear!" over and over again, in a gentle, dismayed way.

Then Jack took it upon himself to address a brief philosophical discourse to the Bishop.

"Everything goes, Bishop," he said; "see? We've got to take things as they come, and if they come mixed, why we've got to take them that way. One day you play in luck; the next you ain't in it, but it all goes—see? If you're all right, that goes. If you get it in the neck, that goes too. That's the way I look at it. I don't know if I know, but that's the way I look at it. Everything goes. Is that right?"

"Unquestionably you are right, Mr. Mc-Marsters," replied the Bishop, "and you do well to remind me of the transitoriness of the annoyances which humanity is too apt to exaggerate into afflictions. But you will pardon an old man's grumbling. Old men," he said, smiling, "are allowed to grumble a little. And I am sure I should be very thankful to have fallen into such good hands."

Then, as he rose from his seat and rested his hand on Jack's arm, he cast a wistful glance at one and the other of our faces, and said, with a gentle dignity that honored us both:

"I am afraid, gentlemen, I may have to ask your indulgence for the infirmities of a very old man—a *very* old man."

We made the Bishop fairly comfortable in the station, and I stayed with him while Jack went in search of a suitable lodging. It seemed a hopeless task, and I began to feel the weight of the responsibility that rested

upon our shoulders. But within half an hour
Jack was back, smiling cheerfully.

"Did you find a hotel?" I asked, eagerly.

"Hotel!" said Jack, contemptuously.
"What place do you think this is, Paris or
Saratoga? There ain't a hotel within ten
miles. But there's a friend of mine keeps a
little sporting place down by the river——"

"A friend of yours!" I exclaimed. "In
this place?"

"Well, I just met him," Jack exclaimed,
calmly, "about fifteen minutes ago. But he
knows me — that is, he knew all about me.
He lost two hundred once on a horse I
owned. He's a first-rate fellow—see? and
he'll take us all in and do for us in elegant
shape."

"Heavens, Jack!" said I, "we can't take
the Bishop to a place like that."

"Yes, we can," said Jack; "it's a first-rate
place. Clean as a new pin. Regular old-
fashioned sporting place. Nice old colored
prints all round. Picture of Hiram Wood-
ruff on one side of the door, and Budd Doble
driving Flora Temple on the other. My
friend and his wife will turn out and give the
Bishop their room, and you and I sleep be-

hind the bar. If any of the boys drop in, he'll see that they're quiet, and there won't be any game to-night—see? Oh, you needn't think I don't know the right thing for a religious swell."

I had my misgivings, but it turned out that Jack had really done very well for us. "Magonigle's" was an absurd little old two-story box on the very edge of the river, evidently a house-of-call for boating and driving men. The whole building was scarcely more than twenty feet square, but the interior was neat and cosey, and the little room upstairs in which we installed the Bishop was simply a delightful little cabin, clean and sweet, and smelling of castile-soap and fresh linen. Magonigle himself was a hearty, kindly little Irishman, and Mrs. Magonigle a motherly, fresh-faced little body, as small for a woman as her husband was for a man. The supper she cooked was, as Jack said, a great deal too good for the Prince of Wales. It was certainly quite good enough for the Bishop. It was broiled spring chicken, fried potatoes, and hot bread, and I shall remember it while I have a palate. Nor shall I forget the India pale ale.

5

After supper Jack put his usual question
to Magonigle :

"Say!" he demanded, "what is there to do
in this town to-night? Now, don't give me
any story about there being nothing. You
know me. There's got to be something."

But Magonigle was firm in his assurances
that there were absolutely no enjoyments to
relieve the monotony of life in Ashe River
Ferry.

"It's a dead place it is, sir. If we could
get over the river I could show you, gentlemen, axing his riverence's pardon, maybe a
bit of a cock-fight, but on this side of the
water there's nothing to see at all, and every
man in the place will be at work the night
long, mending the ferry-boat. 'Tis different
in the summer, sir; but in the winter time
it's just dead this town is."

"Magonigle," said Jack, imperatively,
"turn up *something !*"

Magonigle looked doubtfully at Jack, then
at the Bishop, then at me; and it was to me
that he addressed himself.

"Well, sir," he said, "there's something
what they call a revival meeting going on
out in the woods. There do be some people

takes an interest in such things. They're too sickly like for me, sir, with the women screaming, and having fits, like it might be, on the ground ; but if ye'd like to see it I'd be proud to hitch up the old mare, and it's an easy ride for this part of the country, where the roads is the devil, if I may speak without disrespect for his riverence."

" Niggers ? " inquired Jack.

" No, sir," replied Magonigle. " White folks, such as they are. I don't rightly remember what religion they call themselves ; for it's no church they have here, only meetings like this three or four times in the twelvemonth, maybe."

Jack and I looked at each other. There were limits to even Jack's audacity. We both started as the Bishop's full, deep voice joined in the conversation.

" Gentlemen," said he, " I do not in the least wish to obtrude my society upon you. I feel that I have already given you much trouble ; but, if it does not conflict with your arrangements for this evening, I should very much like to be one of your party. It has never been my fortune to be present at one of these gatherings, and it would deeply

interest me to look on as a spectator. I do
not feel that there can be any impropriety—
and it is a form of worship of which I have
heard much, and which I should like to see
with my own eyes. But, of course, if your
plans——" And he stopped.

"Why, Bishop," said Jack, "we'd sooner
stay here than leave you out. Magoniglo,
hitch up that mare!"

It was eight o'clock when we climbed into
what Magonigle called the carriage—a vehicle
that was neither an express wagon nor a rock-
away, but partook of the nature of both. On
a road so rough that to our Northern understanding it was no road at all, we plunged
into the shadowy, dreary depths of the pine-
wood. The night was clearing, and through
the ragged evergreens we could catch glimpses
of a pale, wind-swept sky. The hot, moist,
sickly smell of the pines and firs half choked
us, the rough bumping of the wagon tired us
and set our nerves on edge, and even Jack
McMarsters had no stomach for talk.

We were all but dazed with weariness of
mind and body, and with the smell of the
resin-laden air, when suddenly a weird flicker
of flaring torches played before our eyes,

dancing slashes of yellow-orange slitting the
deep gloom ahead of us, and dazzling our
sleepy eyes.

Faintly there came to us across the wind,
that whistled and wailed through the trees,
the long-drawn-out notes of a mournful, old-
fashioned hymn, a dismal tune that I knew in
my boyhood. It was one of those sad, stern,
denunciatory old hymns that to my memory
still hold the very spirit of the dead New
England Sabbath in the cheerless, hopeless
melody. The singing ceased for an instant
only ; then there uprose a far greater volume
of voices, tumbling over each other in a mad,
rattling, jingling strain, a popular dance-hall
air, shamelessly and grotesquely twisted into
the form of a hymn. It was a harmless jig-
ging tune enough, but linked to the words
which we could now hear in the lulls of the
wind, it sounded like a profane travesty.

" *He's the Lily of the Valley, the bright and morning*
     star,
  He's the fairest of ten thousand to my soul."

The Bishop turned to me with a look of
troubled surprise.

" Did I catch the meaning of those words ? "

he asked; "or did my ears deceive me? I certainly thought——"

I tried to explain to the Bishop that camp-meeting folk allowed themselves a certain freedom and familiarity in dealing with sacred subjects, which might be in bad taste, but certainly was not ill meant. But he checked me with a touch on my arm.

"Nay, nay," he said, in his old-fashioned manner, "do not misapprehend me. I had not meant to be uncharitable."

"Any tune goes with these people—see?" said Jack, "so long as it is snappy. That's 'The Little Old Log Cabin in the Lane.'"

"Is it, indeed?" said the Bishop.

Magonigle led the way, and we followed him into the circle of wavering, smoking kerosene torches. At first the light dazzled our eyes, but after a few moments we could take note of the picture of gaunt, uncouth poverty around us.

We were in a little clearing of the woods where the stumps had been roughly levelled to serve as supports for heavy, rough-hewn planks, which were the seats. The straggly pines made a black belt around this rude amphitheatre. At the further end was a low

platform of rough timber, where the leaders
of the meeting sat. Here the smoky lamps
were thickest, and they cast a yellow glare on
a little patch of smooth ground that we could
see had been trodden bare by many feet.
Here stood one bench, separate from all the
rest, which might have held a dozen people,
but nobody sat there as we first saw it. Between two and three hundred people were
scattered round among the other benches.
They were all " poor whites," children of the
wilderness, a class apart by themselves ; and
poverty, ignorance, and loneliness stared out
of every sallow face. They all turned to look
at us as we entered, but it was with a vacant,
self-absorbed look, and then their eyes went
back to the platform and the man who stood
on it, or rather walked and leaped and stag-
gered on it.

He was a man between forty and fifty years
of age, with a straggling beard and long hair ;
tall, haggard, and hungry-looking, like the
rest ; but with a light of intelligence in his
face and a consciousness of power in his
bearing that set him above his auditors. He
was accustomed to public speaking ; his voice
was harsh and unpleasant, but strong and

clear, and in spite of its disagreeable quality it had certain curiously caressing and persuasive tones in it. We did not need to study the dumb, brute-like interest of the faces of his hearers to know that this man had laid a spell upon their dull spirits, and that he spoke to each one as if they stood hand-in-hand.

" Oh, my brethren," he cried, raising his long arms high in air, and throwing his lank frame forward in convulsive excitement; "oh, my sisters, the hour is nigh at hand—the hour of grace—the hour of deliverance! For three days have we labored here, for three days have we sought and struggled and prayed for the blessing to come, and no answer has come. But now it's coming, it's coming, it's coming, sinners; I know it's coming! I feel it right here in my heart! Oh, glory, hallelujah! Call with me, all of you, for it's nigh at hand! Salvation's right over you, right by your side! It's touching you right now! Call with me! Oh, Glory! Glory! Glory!"

A few weak cries came up from the outer edges of the throng.

" That won't do," shouted the revivalist,

waving his arms in the air and beating the
platform with his feet, "that won't do! I
want you all to shout with me! I want you
to shout so that the Lord hears you! Now
once more! Glory! Glory!"

"Glory!" thundered Jack McMarsters,
next to me.

"Be quiet, you devil," I whispered, grasp-
ing him by the arm.

"Got to help them out," said Jack.
"Glory! Glory!"

And as his big voice rang out upon the air
the whole crowd followed him as if a sudden
madness had seized them, and the torches
flickered as one wild, deafening shout of
"Glory! Glory! Glory!" rose up to the
bleak sky.

The sweat poured down the preacher's face
as he joined in the shout, quivering from
head to foot.

"That's it!" he fairly yelled. "I knew it
was coming! I knew it had to come! Now,
who is the first to come forward? Who is
the first to come to this bench? Who is the
first to come to this throne of glory and be
born again? Oh, don't wait, don't linger an
instant, or the moment may be forever lost!

Hell eternal or eternal life! Who is the first?
Who is the first to save a soul from eternal
hell?"

He stretched his arms out as if he were
feeling for something in space. Suddenly
the long fore-finger of his right hand pointed
directly at a sickly looking woman on a
near-by bench.

"Oh, my sister!" he cried out, "do you
feel it? has it come to you? Are you the
first on whom the Lord has descended?
Come forward, come forward! Come to the
seat of those who wait for the Lord—come!"

The woman arose, and slowly and feebly,
her eyes fixed on the face of the preacher,
she came forward as one who had no power
to resist.

"I knew it, I knew it!" the revivalist
shouted. "Come forward, my sister, and
when you have touched that blessed bench
grace will come to you as your soul wrestles
in agony. I can see it working. I can see
the hand of the Lord upon you!"

The woman reached the bench as he spoke,
and touched it with her thin, quivering hand,
and a hysterical shriek, horrible to hear,
burst from her. Every figure in the crowd

behind her bent forward, and cries of " Glory! Glory!" rent the air. But none came from Jack this time, for the woman was lying on her back across the bench, her poor, thin form writhing and twisting, clasping and unclasping her hands until her nails tore the worn flesh.

I looked on with a shuddering sickness. My brain whirled. I could not make myself believe that it was real, that it was true, that I saw this thing going on before my eyes. Then I became conscious of a sensation of acute physical pain, and, looking down, I saw that the Bishop had grasped my wrist, and that his strong fingers had closed on it in a grip that seemed to drive the flesh into the bone. I understood what that grasp meant when I looked at his face. He was pale as death, and the features were fixed in a stern. ness that struck cold to my heart.

And all this time the revivalist shouted to the sobbing, swaying crowd.

"Come," he cried, "come, all who would be saved from hell! Here is one who has the grace. Who will join her? Who will save his soul to-night? This is the only way, and this may be the only moment! Who comes forward for salvation?"

The Bishop was breathing heavily, with long, trembling breaths, but I noticed that his expression had changed. It was no longer stern. It was strange and sad, and his look was fixed on something far away— far beyond the blackness of the black woods behind the madman who shrieked upon the platform. I felt a sudden fear, and turned toward Jack.

He was not by my side. I looked round and saw him at the rail that enclosed the clearing. He was placing a white-faced child in a woman's arms, and I saw by his gestures that he was forcing her to leave that place of horror. In a moment he was back, and, with one glance at me, he sat down on the other side of the Bishop and laid his steady hand on the old man's arm.

"Come!" screamed the man on the platform. "Come and choose between the Lord and hell! Every soul here is hanging over the fires of hell eternal. Come and be saved!"

But already, on the bench, under it, and on all sides of it lay a score of struggling, agonized human beings, beating the ground, tearing their very flesh in the exaltation of fear and frenzy, choking, gasping; and through it all, shrieking mad and awful appeals to the Most High; while the crowd around them, all on their feet, shouted and yelled in incoherent delirium.

"Come! come!" the voice on the platform rose above the din. "Be saved while there is yet time."

"ALMIGHTY GOD——"

My heart stood still. The Bishop had risen to his feet, and his gigantic figure towered up as he spread out his hands above the crowd; and, as his deep tones rang out clear and dominant in that hideous Babel, a sudden silence fell upon them all.

"——THE FATHER OF OUR LORD JESUS CHRIST, WHO DESIRETH NOT THE DEATH OF A SINNER, BUT RATHER THAT HE MAY TURN FROM HIS WICKEDNESS AND LIVE, HATH GIVEN POWER, AND COMMANDMENT, TO HIS MINISTERS, TO DECLARE AND PRONOUNCE TO HIS PEOPLE, BEING PENITENT, THE ABSOLUTION AND REMISSION OF THEIR SINS. HE PARDONETH AND ABSOLVETH ALL THOSE WHO TRULY REPENT, AND UNFEIGNEDLY BELIEVE HIS HOLY GOSPEL."

The madness had gone—utterly gone—out of that stricken throng. The struggling fig-

ures around the bench ceased to struggle.
They raised their heads as they lay upon the
ground, and every face in the clearing was
turned toward the Bishop, wearing a look of
eager wonderment which I shall never forget.
The Bishop, his eyes still far away, his hands
stretched out over the people, went on :

"——WHEREFORE LET US BESEECH HIM TO
GRANT US TRUE REPENTANCE, AND HIS HOLY
SPIRIT, THAT THOSE THINGS MAY PLEASE HIM
WHICH WE DO AT THIS PRESENT ; AND THAT THE
REST OF OUR LIFE HEREAFTER MAY BE PURE
AND HOLY ; SO THAT AT THE LAST WE MAY COME
TO HIS ETERNAL JOY ; THROUGH JESUS CHRIST
OUR LORD."

And the people answered, " Amen."

When he had finished he steadied himself
by my shoulder, at first with a nervous pressure ; but in a moment I felt the tension of
his muscles relax. Then, in a voice that was
almost feeble, so tender had it grown, he
turned toward the East, and, in that abiding
silence, he pronounced the Benediction.

For a moment, until they began to disperse
softly and silently, the Bishop stood erect,
then he sank back into his seat, with one arm
around my neck and one around Jack's.

"THE BISHOP, HIS EYES STILL FAR AWAY, HIS HANDS STRETCHED OUT
OVER THE PEOPLE, WENT ON"

CRAZY WIFE'S SHIP

CRAZY WIFE'S SHIP

"I CAN'T see for the rain. Who—that there going up the hill? Why, I thought you knew most everybody on the island by this time! I'd have thought you'd known *her*, anyway. Why, that's old Mis' Bint—the aunt of all that tribe of Bints that live just near Calais. No, Mr. Woglom, that isn't the least bit what I was looking for. That isn't pa'm leaf—anyway, not what we used to call pa'm leaf. Why, now, it's strange you don't know Mis' Bint—and you so well acquainted around here too. Why, you had ought to write her up in some of your papers —hadn't he, Mr. Woglom? It's quite some of a story, if only anybody knew how to fix it up the right way, sost it would go in the newspapers. Why, I should have thought you'd have remarked her mourning!"

I could not help remarking her mourning now, at all events. I watched her struggling

6

up the bleak island hillside, passing in and out of sight among the scraggly pines; and such a grimly fantastic figure, so swathed and swaddled and hung about and decked on with crape and stiff old-fashioned black stuffs, I had never before seen. Her veil projected on each side of her head as though her big old-fashioned bonnet were rigged out with stun-sail booms. The wind buffeted her; the rain drenched her in angry little spats, first to starboard and then to port, but she tacked steadily on up the hill, with all her voluminous garments flapping bravely, as stiff and black as sheet-iron. I was watching her through the one clear pane in the window of Mr. Woglom's general store. Tarpaulins, rubber boots, sou'westers, fishing-tackle, scap-nets, school-books, suspenders, overalls, garden tools, horse medicine, mosquito-netting, lanterns, and other general-store stock, including the accursed lottery ticket, which is for sale in Maine everywhere where anything is sold, filled up the rest of the window. I was waiting for the squall to blow over. Miss Cynthiana Lovejoy, who accommodated me with board and lodging during my stay on the island, had happened in and was casually examining the new invoice of calicoes from New York, in search, Mr. Woglom confidentially told me, of a pattern which she had wanted for at least a generation, and which had been two generations out of the market.

"Now what year was it, do you remember, Mr. Woglom, when Obed Bint's ship was lost in that gale when the big whale come ashore? No, I don't mean Isaac Bint; I mean Obed Bint, Isaac's son—the young man—that is, he wouldn't be so dreadful young to-day if he'd lived—most fifty now, I should think. Mr. Woglom, that ain't any more pa'm leaf than I'm pa'm leaf.

"Sixty-seven? Well, now, I wouldn't have thought it was so far back as sixty-seven. Land's sake, how time does go! Yes, that's something like the pattern, but 'tisn't just *it*. Only I can't draw at all, I could draw that pattern for you just as clear as day. Well, now, it doesn't seem so long. But I guess you're right, Mr. Woglom. That was just the year that I bought the first piece of magenta poplin I ever saw, off your father. My, I thought I was made! Father, he used to call it my whale dress, because he paid for

it out of the money he made off that whale.
It came ashore right on his beach.

"That was a real bad storm, Mr. Woglom, if you recollect. Let me see—there
was Obed Bint's boat, and Plum Davis's
boat, and the two Daw brothers, their boat,
and that man who lived on Three Acre
Island, what was his name, now?—oh, yes,
Wilkinson—well, there was his boat, too;
not a one of them came back. Every one
of those boats was lost in that gale. At
least, not a one of them ever came in. Awful, wa'n't it?

"Well, now, what I was going to tell you
about Mis' Bint that was so queer was just
this, and I thought you might make sort of a
story of it, if you could only fix it up some
way sost it would read well. It was this
way. Obed, he married just before he made
his first trip on his own boat—married a girl
he met at Eastport the year he went over
there to go to a dancing-school they had there
—'twa'n't much of a concern, I guess, but it
was the best they was. She was a real nice
little thing, and pretty too, and clever to
everybody. She made friends with lots of
people. I remember it was real gay on the

island that year; there was two or three other young married couples too.

"Well, as I was telling you, that big whale —my! he was a monstrous big thing!—that whale came up on our beach the same gale Obed Bint's boat was lost in. And of course we had to attend to the whale right off, and cut him up before he'd spoil, and—I don't know—but it took quite some time, and in consequence we didn't get over to see Mis' Bint as much as we had ought to; 'twa'n't that we didn't want to; but there was the whale, don't you see?

"Dear me, Mr. Woglom, I can remember that magenta dress just the same as if it was yesterday! I remember how I bought it off your father on this very counter. I remember just what he says when he sold it to me. Says he, 'You'll look just like that piny bed up to Widow Pierson's when you get that on,' says he. Why, it wa'n't no more like the color of pinies than nothing at all. Your father hadn't what folks call an eye for color, Mr. Woglom.

"Now, what *was* I saying? Oh yes! I know! I had that magenta dress on the first day that I ever looked across the cove from

my father's house to the meadow lot under
the light-house, and saw Mis' Bint and
Obed's wife setting there looking out to sea
as if they's expecting something. My great-
grandmother, my father's grandmother, that
is, she was alive then, and she was a real
queer old lady. She'd sit in an old splint-bot-
tomed chair by the chimney all day long and
never say a word—only set bolt-upright and
smoke an old corn-cob pipe just like a man.
I don't know what made me speak to her
when I saw Mis' Bint and Obed's wife settin'
there under the light-house, but I did, somehow. Says I, 'Granny, there's Mis' Bint
and Obed's wife under the light-house looking out to sea. What do you think they're
looking for?' says I.

"'Crazy wife's ship,' says she, short, just
like that, and she didn't say another thing
that day. That was a way she had; she
didn't often say anything, but when she did
say something she was real curious.

"I don't know whether it was an old-
fashioned saying or something she made up
herself, but it gave me a real sort of a turn.
And that afternoon I went over to Mis' Bint's,
that is, my mother and I did. They lived

quite a piece away on the other side of the
cove, but our two families had always been
first-rate friends, and my father had taught
Obed Bint all he knew about navigation.
Well, you may imagine it took us all aback
when old Mis' Bint met us at the gate, and
we saw right away that she wa'n't going
to let us in. That was the first time I ever
saw or heard of neighbors quarrelling on the
island—I've seen enough since, but I was only
a young slip of a girl then, and it did seem
perfectly dreadful to me. Mis' Bint she
talked—oh, she talked quite violently, and
reproached us for not coming sooner, and as
much as said she wanted to have done with
us for good and all. My mother—she was a
very proud woman—she never answered her
back at all, but she just took me by the hand
and told me to come along, and we started
for home. I didn't dare say anything; I was
most too frightened to speak. And mother
she didn't say a word, but just walked right
on leading me by the hand as if I was a
baby.

"Going back we met old Mr. Starbuck, the
one who used to live in the red house down
by the Point. He was about the only near

neighbor the Bints had—between 'em I guess they owned pretty much all that end of the island.

" 'Hello!' says he, when he saw my mother. 'Been to call on me?'

" 'What do you mean, Mr. Starbuck?' says my mother, for she didn't know what to make of his asking such a question.

" 'Why,' he says, 'I supposed you'd been to my house. I understand folks ain't admitted anywheres else in this neighborhood.'

" We didn't understand him just then, but we did when we got down to the village and heard the talk that was going on. You never heard anything so queer in all your life. It was a real nine-days' wonder, as the saying is. It seemed that old Mis' Bint had picked a quarrel with everybody on the island, on one pretext or another, so that there wa'n't one that she hadn't, so to speak, shut her doors on. Dreadful queer behavior! With one it was one thing and with another it was something different, but it all came to pretty much the same in the end—she wa'n't on speaking terms with hardly a soul in the place, and there she was, living up on the Point with not a neighbor to go near her, mewed up

all alone there with Melindy—that was
Obed's wife's name. Everybody was sorry
for the poor little clever creature, for Mis'
Bint wa'n't a cheerful woman the best of
times, and when she *was* vexed, *my !* she
was vexed.

" But then, of course, we couldn't do anything, she kept Melindy so close—wouldn't
let her stir anywheres without her, and it
got so at last that she wouldn't hardly let
her go out at all.

"Of course we all made out that the loss
of her son had turned her mind, and people
was all the more sorry for Melindy on that
account. She pined away dreadfully too ;
lost all her good looks, and got real peaked.

" For one thing, her mother-in-law would
never let her wear mourning, nor Mis' Bint
wouldn't wear a stitch of black herself. That's
what made folks say she was crazy first off; for
though there's lots of people here who won't
wear mourning clothes on principle, old Mis'
Bint come from Calais, and she was a Bint
by birth, too, before she married Isaac Bint;
and all those Bints, the whole stock of them,
were just *sot* on dressing all out in black,
every cousin that died. She was real par-

ticular about her dress, Mis' Bint was. I
think folks was generally more particular in
those days. I know there ain't any patterns
nowadays like that old pa'm-leaf pattern ; not
so nice, that is, to my taste.

"Of course Mis' Bint didn't drop out like
that without being considerable missed. Melindy was kind of new to the town, but her
mother-in-law was a good deal looked up to.
She was a great housekeeper for one thing,
and when there was anything going on—I
mean sociably—weddings and funerals, for
instance, people always use to a sort of de-
pend on Mis' Bint. And then she was a
master-hand at nursing sick folks and taking care of young children, and altogether
people missed her—quite some. Mr. Woglom, if you can't show me those dress goods
yourself, don't bother to put that boy of
yours at it, for you just might as well not. I
don't believe he knows gingham from goose-
grease.

"Let me see, I guess it must have been
two-three years, maybe four, that I found
out the rights of the matter, and just acci-
dently, as you might say. The light-house I
was telling you about was away at the far

end of the Point, and nobody hardly ever
went there, except, of course, the man who
kept the light, and he was a Portugee or
something—some kind of a foreigner anyway, and didn't talk much English. But ever
since she began to act so queer, old Mis'
Bint had made a regular practice of going
down there and setting with her daughter-in-
law—oh, my! for hours at a time, and every
day, too, in all sorts of weather. I don't believe anybody knew about it, though, except
our folks, for you could see them where they
sat from our kitchen window, but not from
much of any place else. And as for my
mother, from the day old Mis' Bint spoke
sharp to her to the day of her death, she
never mentioned the name of Bint, and you
may believe I wouldn't have dared to mention it to *her*. The way it happened was
this, and it was kind of funny. I had a little green parrot about *that* long. A sailor
uncle of mine brought it to me from Java,
somewheres in the tropics—my Uncle Hiram,
one of my mother's folks; he died young,
and I guess there ain't anybody remembers
him now, without it's me, and I don't believe
I'd ever think of him if it wa'n't for that par-

rot.   It was a cute little thing, and I set a
heap by it, though it couldn't talk, and it was
dreadful mis*chie*vous.   It died, in the end,
of swallowing a needle-book.   Well, as I was
saying, that bird got loose one awful bleak
day in November, and ran right along the
shore of the cove, and made straight to Bint's
place, and me after it, you'd better believe,
running just as hard as I could tear.   And
you wouldn't have thought a little thing could
get over such a lot of ground so amazing fast.
It was clean over in Mis' Bint's cow-pasture
before I caught it, and then I started for
home real frightened, for I didn't know what
my mother would say to me if she ever knew
I'd been anywheres on land belonging to the
Bints.   She was dreadful strict sometimes,
my mother was.

"Well, just by good luck, nobody saw me,
and I come back by the short-cut across the
Point under the light-house.   And would you
believe it, just as I got under that sand bank
there with the swallows' nests in it—you can
see 'em from here—that dratted parrot got
away from me again ; and I was so tuckered
out what with the running and the fright and
the disappointment and all that—it sounds

kinder foolish now, don't it?—I just laid
right down there on the sand and cried as if
I was going to cry my eyes out.

"And while I was lying there and crying
fit to break my heart, the first thing I knew I
heard people's voices talking on the bank
above me. I couldn't see them, and at first
I thought it was some of our folks come after
me, and I was worse scared than ever, and
just laid quiet, not knowing what *to* do. Then
I recognized Mis' Bint's voice and Melindy's,
though, as I say, I hadn't spoken a word to
either of them in three-four years, but you
may fancy it sent a real cold chill down my
back when I heard old Mis' Bint say, in a
perfectly peaceful, ca'm, natural way, just as
I am talking to you now:

"'No, dearie; Obed can't get in on that
wind. He'll most likely lay to on t'other
side of South Island, and come up with the
tide in the morning.'

"'But he'll come in the morning sure,
won't he, ma?' says Melindy; and it gave
me an awful funny creepy feeling to hear her,
for she talked a sort of innocent, something
like a little child.

'"Oh yes,' says old Mis' Bint. 'Obed will

come in the morning sure. You'd better be thinking of getting a good breakfast for him.'

" ' Yes,' says Melindy ; ' picked-up codfish. Obed always was great for picked-up codfish.'

"Well, if I was scared before, I was scared worse than ever now. Why, it was just the unnaturalist thing that you ever could form a notion of, setting there and hearing those two women talking about getting breakfast for a man who had been lying four years at the bottom of the sea. It 'most made my blood run cold ; but of course I didn't dare to stir, and I just *had* to set there and listen while they laid out the breakfast they was going to get ready for him—picked-up codfish and mock mince-pie and I don't know what all. And then they talked about how soon he'd be rested enough to feel like taking a journey up the river to Bucksport to pay a visit to his Uncle John. My! his Uncle John 'd been dead two years.

" I don't know what it was I did at last that attracted their attention. I guess I must have coughed or something, because Mis' Bint she called out suddenly, ' What's that? ' and looked over the sand bank and saw me.

I wasn't so scared then but what I got straight
up and started to run. But Mis' Bint she just
came down and caught me by the arm, and
walked me quite a ways down the beach before she said a word. Then she talked right
close to my ear sost I could hear her, but
Melindy couldn't.

"'You think I'm a lunatic,' she says.

"'Yes, ma'am,' I says. I didn't know what
to say, but I was a real truthful child.

"'Well, I ain't,' says Mis' Bint. 'I'm as
sane as you are. But *she's* an idiot, and she's
been so ever since the night of the big gale;
and I've kep' up the delusion in her mind that
Obed's coming home,' says she. 'I've encouraged her in it, because if I didn't she
wouldn't live a week.'

"Then she looked at me real hard for
a minute, and then she said:

"'That's why I don't want folks around.
You're John Lovejoy's daughter, ain't you?'
says she.

"'Yes, ma'am,' says I.

"'Well,' says she, 'you've seen the afflic-
tion the Lord's visited upon me. Now what
you going to do? Tell folks?'

"Then I spunked up. I guess she knew I

would. 'Mis' Bint,' says I, 'I guess our folks 'ain't meddled with your affairs very lately, and I don't think,' says I, 'that we're going to begin now,' I told her. And with that I walked away. I was real mad.

"And do you know, it was the funniest thing. I hadn't gone more than a hundred yards when what should I see but that parrot a-hopping along in front of me, heading for home across the sand. He was dreadful little, but I could see him a long ways off; he was such a bright green against the beach, and the day was kinder gray too, sost he showed up quite some. It was a green something like that pattern, Mr. Woglom, but with more yellow into it.

"And I never did say one word about it for the longest time. But maybe three-four years after that Melindy fell kind of sick, and they had to send for a doctor, and then somehow it all came out. But it didn't do any harm, I guess, for Melindy wa'n't sick long. She died that January, and the first boat that got through the ice to the mainland that spring old Mis' Bint went over on it to Eastport, and when she come back she had the greatest lot of mourning clothes that

I guess most any woman ever had. She's taken some of it off since then, and they don't wear skirts so full now, so you don't notice it so much, but still she wears considerable— enough to notice, I should think. But they do say she's a great deal more sociable now— though, my! I don't know. *I* 'ain't spoken to her since.

"No, Mr. Woglom," concluded Miss Cynthiana, as she felt the edge of the last piece of calico between her thumb and her forefinger, " you needn't trouble yourself to show me anything more. I don't believe you've got the real pa'm leaf anyway. Though I was in hopes you might have had it, you've talked so much of getting it for me so many times. Does Mis' Bint buy her mourning of you now, or does she still go to Eastport for it? But wa'n't it curious, my finding that parrot again that way?"

Between the legs of a pendent pair of wading-boots I peered out of the dripping window, looking at the crest of the storm-swept hill, and caught a last glimpse of the gaunt black figure tacking against the wind, funereal and lonely.

7

FRENCH FOR A FORTNIGHT

FRENCH FOR A FORTNIGHT

"OH, dear!" said the Reverend Mr. Pentagon. "Oh, dear! Oh, dear! Oh, dear!"

Then he tossed uneasily upon his neat white bed, and ground his broad shoulders into its snowy depths. He looked out of the window, and saw, through the pale green panes of flint glass a bough of darker green bob up and down, shaking off great drops of rain as the last gust of the summer rainstorm agitated it and gently subsided. Beyond, the gray sky, that had but now been weeping, was slowly growing blue; not smiling yet, but tearfully clearing up to tranquil brightness. To people not in an unpleasant frame of mind it might have suggested the face of a child coming out of a crying spell. To the Reverend Mr. Pentagon, who was in a

very unpleasant frame of mind, it suggested
nothing beyond the fact that he had to wait
before he could walk out under the blue sky.
He stared and tossed, and stared and tossed
again, and once more he said, explosively :

"Oh, dear!"

If the Recording Angel sets down our
words according to what they mean to our
hearts rather than by their dictionary meaning, he credited the Reverend Mr. Pentagon's account with a right, good, healthy bit
of profanity on the score of that last "Oh,
dear!" And, indeed, if he had said some awful
thing with "Damn" in it, he could not have
meant anything worse. For the Reverend
Mr. Pentagon was lying in bed and thinking
of the days that had dropped out of his life
during a long period of unconsciousness and
delirium.

"Fifteen days," he said to himself. "Fifteen days! Oh, dear! Oh, dear! Oh,
dear!"

.   .   .   .

The Reverend Mr. Pentagon was a clergyman of culture and understanding, who, writing and preaching from a small provincial
city in Massachusetts, had made a name for

himself all over the country, and indeed wherever the old Church of England points its
spires toward the sky, or drops earthward the
clangor of its square belfries. So great had
grown his fame that when he gave up the
charge he had held for fifteen years, being forced thereto by ill health, and, going into the Canada woods, was, in the
course of one summer, recovered of fifteen
years of dyspepsia, why, it so happened that
this modest provincial parson found himself
given to understand that if a certain series of
sermons which he was invited to deliver in
New York should please the congregation to
whom they were addressed, he would in all
probability be called to fill the pulpit of one
of the great city's fashionable churches. It
was a very old, a very rich, a very exclusive
church. The old Rector was about to resign
by reason of his age : not wholly to the regret of certain members of his congregation,
who found that in the years of his steward-
ship the dear old gentleman had " slowly
broadened down from precedent to precedent " until he was almost as broad and charitable as the New Testament itself. So, naturally, they wanted a man who, if he had to

broaden down, would start from a higher plane of orthodoxy, and such a man they were sure they had found in the Reverend Mr. Pentagon.

So, too, Mr. Pentagon thought, and he came down from the Canada woods, and in a pretty little town among the rocks of the Maine coast set himself to write his series of sermons. There were to be six in the series, but I know the heads of only three of them. The first was "On the Reciprocal Duties of the Church and the Pastor." The second was "On the Duty of Church-going." The third was entitled, "On the Duty of a Strict Observance of the Sabbath."

It was while he was writing this sermon that the Reverend Mr. Pentagon chanced to ask himself whether it would not be well for the rector of a New York church to know something about New York. He had had enough acquaintance with Boston, which he considered a large city, to grasp the idea that large cities have ways of their own which they are not at all inclined to change at the pleasure of the casual stranger. Moreover, Mr. Pentagon was a man whose native habit of mind was liberal enough, and he happened to be free

from the usual intolerant provincial hatred of
big cities. And he made up his mind that he
would go at once, all by himself, to see what
New York was like. He had been in New
York, of course, but only to stay for a few
days at a boarding-house with a delegation of
his own townspeople at the time of a great
convention of the Church.

He knew that New York was almost intol-
erably hot in summer-time, and so he con-
ceived for himself the notion of a resting-
place in the suburbs, from whence he could
make brief incursions into the body of the
town, coming back at night to the green fields
and fresh air. He consulted with his brother
of the local church, a Portland man who had
been in New York in 1874, who gave him just
the address he wanted—a nice, quiet little
place in Westchester County, on the Bronx
River, where he could board most comforta-
bly at next to nothing.

Clergymen are wonderfully like sheep in
many things. The Reverend Mr. Pentagon
packed a large old-fashioned travelling bag—
of course—and set out for the nice place on the
Bronx River. He found it readily enough,
for there was only one other house within five

miles. It had been an excellent house, but it was now getting along without doors or windows, in a sad and paintless old age. The family that had entertained his clerical friend so hospitably in the year 1874, had moved out in the year 1875, and the house had had no tenant since. This much he learned of the man of the other house, who was a fat and kindly French tavern-keeper, with the reddest of faces and the whitest of aprons, and an amount of politeness that made the Reverend Mr. Pentagon feel more awkward than he had felt since he was a little boy at school and got up on the platform to speak his little piece just as the four awful school inspectors dropped in on a sudden visit of inspection. On that occasion, he remembered, his little bare legs felt as if they had ten joints in each one of them, and he certainly had fourteen fingers on each hand.

As awkward as a child and as lonely as a lost child, the Reverend Mr. Pentagon stood in front of the house of Monsieur Perot and stared blankly at the inn and at the landlord until an idea slowly crept into his mind. The inn looked very clean and neat. It was an odd little old-fashioned structure with green

WHY MIGHT NOT THE REVEREND MR. PENTAGON TAKE LODGINGS AT THE
INN OF MONSIEUR PEROT?

palings and trellises stuck about it in various places, and it overhung the margin of the placid Bronx and mirrored its whitewashed front in the calm stream. The landlord's face inspired confidence—so, too, did a smell of crisp, clean cooking that came from the kitchen of Madame Perot. Why might not the Reverend Mr. Pentagon take lodgings at the inn of Monsieur Perot? There was no reason why he might not, and in the end he did.

Very comfortable he found himself, and very friendly were the *famille Perot;* and a multitudinous family they were. Mr. Pentagon never succeeded in taking the census of them all, which need not be wondered at when it is said that the eleventh infant of Monsieur and Madame Perot was exactly of the same age as the third child of their first married daughter. And all of them, of every age and size, were polite by birth and inheritance, and took a cheerful view of life.

The first day of his arrival, which was a Saturday, Mr. Pentagon took out his unfinished sermon, meaning to set to work. Then he read it over, and it struck him that really it was so very strong, especially the passage in denunciation of the Continental Sabbath, that he really ought to wait until he found himself in just the proper spirit to go on with it. He had a feeling of chastened pride in the thought that he had denounced that sinful Continental Sabbath very aptly indeed for a man who had never seen it. So that day he went for a walk and saw some of the pretty places which are too near to New York for most New Yorkers to visit. The next day was Sunday, and he went into the City and worshipped at Trinity, and on his way home went out of his course to view the great church to which he expected to be called, and stood and looked at its closed doors; and his heart beat hard.

On Monday he went to New York again, and again on Tuesday, and again on Wednesday, and again on Thursday. Hither and thither he wandered, bewildered at first, then fascinated. The cosmopolitan variety of the life amazed and interested him. He had a slight book-knowledge of several languages, and in his ramblings he heard them all and many that he could not recognize. On Friday he stumbled on the Polish quarter in Attorney Street and thereabouts, and then,

strolling aimlessly on, got into Mulberry
Bend and was suddenly seized with a nervous
fright at the swarming vastness of that mighty
ant-hill. He gazed about him at the count-
less foreign faces that streamed this way and
that through the narrow pass; he blinked at
the marvellous street-stands with their wild
confusion of reds and greens and whites; he
looked up at the thin strip of blue sky between the tops of the towering tenements;
and then his eye fell upon the huge form of
the Irish policeman who sauntered grandly
through all this bustle and turmoil of agile
Italians, and he said to him:

"Do you think that any of these people
would offer me violence if I were to proceed
farther along this street?"

The policeman looked down at him kindly,
but from an infinite height of scorn.

"An' ME here?" he said.

Mr. Pentagon went on unmolested, and
before he had reached the end of the street
he had some glimmering realization of the
fact that it was not only the big policeman
who was keeping order for him, but the spirit
of good-natured, happy, all-expectant indus-
try that is the salvation of the poor whose

feet are on the road that may lead to prosperity if they will but keep to it. But not then, not till long, long afterward, did Mr. Pentagon learn the awful difference between the hopeful and the hopeless poor.

.   .   .   .

Friday found the Reverend Mr. Pentagon tired and footsore, with not one word added to the sermon "On the Duty of a Strict Observance of the Sabbath." Then, having lain on his lounge all day Friday, of course he needed a little exercise on Saturday. He thought he would take a row. He had rowed at college, and once or twice on the broad river that ran by the town that had been his home for fifteen years.

But he had never rowed on the Bronx, and the Bronx is a river that requires a special education for its navigation. It winds, it twists, it turns, it doubles upon itself, it spreads out into a pond, it contracts to a mere thread of water; in fact it is the most capricious and absurd little water-course on the face of the civilized globe.

And so it happened that Mr. Pentagon, coming around a turn with an unnecessarily powerful stroke, and with his body thrown

back, ran into a stone bridge, struck his
head full on the spring of the arch, and went
backward into his boat, unconscious of everything in this world, save a dim sense of grind-
ing pain, and of alternate heat and chill.

After this came a long period when he had
a certain fitful knowledge of things and people about him. He saw faces—the faces of
the elder members of the Perot family, the
red good-natured face of Monsieur Perot, the
kindly withered face of his old wife, the sweet
and pretty face of the married daughter; now
and then wondering faces of children looking
in at the doorway, and at certain regular intervals a man's face, grave and gentle, with
searching eyes that were somehow connected
in his mind with the word "Doctor."

Then came the time when he awoke to
know that he had been sick nigh unto death,
and out of his head, and out of this world
more or less, for a period of days. When he
asked how many, the Doctor answered him
evasively, and he fretted over the evasion
with all the futile insistence of a convales-
cent. He could learn nothing from Madame
Perot, who could have made a professional
cross-examiner change any given subject for

any other one he did not want. But at last he caught Monsieur Perot and bullied him into an admission. Perot would not absolutely defy the Doctor's orders, but in the end, being in an agony of perspiration and trepidation, he told Mr. Pentagon that he might calculate the rest for himself; it was now fifteen days since the reverend gentleman had honored the house with his presence.

"Quinze jours," said the Reverend Mr. Pentagon to himself, "Saturday, Sunday, Monday, Tuesday"—and he went on counting on his fingers. "Why, to-day must be Sunday!"

Even as he spoke a church bell tinkled faintly in the distance. It tinkled long enough to remind the Reverend Mr. Pentagon that instead of scolding at the week that lay before him, it behooved him to thank the Lord for his deliverance, and he accordingly did so, without the aid of his Book of Common Prayer; for his injury had somewhat endangered his eyesight, and he was absolutely forbidden to read.

. . . .

Mr. Pentagon was a strong, healthy, temperate man; and he made a most rapid recovery. To be more exact it was soon to be seen that his case would have no *sequelæ*, as the good, grave Doctor loved to call the secondary consequences of an ailment. Instead of a week, he was kept but a day longer in bed, and two days in his room, and after that he was allowed to wander the whole day long under Monsieur Perot's cherry-trees, or to sun himself on the little veranda overlooking the stream. He could not read, which tried him a little, but his young friends of the innumerable tribe of Perot made life bearable, in fact, delightful for him. His French, what there was of it, was of what might be called the passive sort; and he understood perhaps one word in three of what the elder Perots said to him. But the children, as is often the case with Franco-American youngsters, spoke two languages with equal fluency and incorrectness, and moreover combined the two as they saw fit. Thus Mr. Pentagon conversed with them in a sort of Pigeon-English, or lingua franca, after this fashion:

MR. PENTAGON.—Kee ay ploorong, Mahree?

MARIE ANGÉLIQUE EULALIE ROSE ÉTIENNE PEROT (*aged seven*).—Mais, m'sieu, c'est Toto qui pleure, parce qu'il a tveesté la tail à la chatte, et puis papa lui a fetchée des gifles."

That's what the beautiful language of France comes to on the banks of the winding Bronx.

. . . .

Mr. Pentagon had never married, he had no near kin, and he was not in the habit of keeping up close correspondence with even the best of his many friends. But when he awoke on the third morning of his convalescence as an *externe*, he reflected that he must very soon find some way of notifying those who cared for him of his present condition and whereabouts. He thought he would ask the Doctor, who still came to see him once a day, if he would not write the requisite letters for him. The Doctor was a serious man, his face was almost sad in its thoughtfulness, and he was chary of speech to the verge of taciturnity; but there was an earnest kindliness in his thoughtful eyes which made Mr. Pentagon feel sure that he would write the letters, and would write them well.

Much cheered by this conclusion he finished his dressing and was about to start downstairs, when the door opened and he beheld Monsieur Perot, in gorgeous attire, with a large tri-colored bouquet in his buttonhole ; Madame Perot in her very best dress with a marvellous and complicated white cap on her gray head, and the married daughter, with her husband, both costumed in the most advanced art of the Bowery. Behind them, like the incidental cherubs with which the Old Masters used to fill up the odd corners of their canvases, surged a selected group of small Perots, the girls all in white dresses with big sashes, and the boys all in white shirts with tri-colored neckties.

There was a flood, a deluge, an explosion of French, and after Mr. Pentagon had struggled with it for some time, and had been helped out by the younger members of the delegation, he got it through his head that he was invited to join the Perot family at the Summer Festival of the French Society to which they belonged, this festival being a combined fête and pique-nique at Tompkinson's Summer-Garden Park, a paradise of unspeakable delights situated in the immediate neighborhood.

It would have been impossible for Mr. Pentagon to refuse, if he had wished to refuse, which he did not in the least.

"I ought to see about the letters," he reflected; "but then, this being Saturday, they could not go until Monday, and I need miss only a single mail. And really I must not lose this opportunity of seeing what a French Festival is like."

Three country stages of vast age and of unlimited capacity transported the Perot family through clouds of dust to Mr. Tompkinson's Garden, which was shut off from the rest of the world by a high yellow fence. Through a gateway decked with the fluttering flags of all nations and of several defunct yacht-clubs, the party was whirled, in such a tumult of joyous shouting and shrieking as Mr. Pentagon had never in his life heard before. His head whirled with it, and it was with the sense of being in a dream that he found himself seated at a table under a tree, drinking a milky sweet stuff called orgeat, and by the aid of a spoon sharing his beverage with a warm and sticky little Perot, who had perched on his left knee. In front of them a company of eleven amateur soldiers, attired in

MR. PENTAGON OPENED HIS EYES WIDE TO TAKE IN THE UNACCUSTOMED
SCENE

uniforms that would have made Solomon in all his glory look like a Quaker, performed evolutions of a mysterious and rapid nature, looking extremely fierce all the while, and thumping the butts of their guns on the ground every now and then, with a snort of defiance. This done, they mopped their hot faces, accepted the congratulations of the Perot family with smiling satisfaction, took off their hats and bowed in the politest way, and went off somewhere else to do it again.

In every direction somebody was doing something. The "Park" was a poor bare place, with dusty trees, and dry and faded grass, and the little booths that lined its yellow walls were old and weatherbeaten, and their sparse decorations of red, white, and blue bunting were pitifully faded with sun and rain. But the people made it gay—the swarms of happy holidaying folk, some of them in quaint, old-world costumes, some of them in brilliant uniforms of designs that would have looked equally strange on either side of the water—all of them wearing hot and smiling faces. Mr. Pentagon opened his eyes wide to take in the unaccustomed scene. The women's caps were wonderful to him; so were the waistcoats of the men. As to the various sports and games, he had never dreamed that there were so many ways of amusing one's self in the world. There were shooting-galleries, and merry-go-rounds, and "Aunt Sallies," and the tiniest little switch-back railway, which was labelled in letters as big as itself, "*Aux Montagnes Russes.*" And in every little open space of the extensive grounds there was a club or a society, or a league, or a group, or some other aggregation of from six to a dozen young men, practising some athletic sports with infinite perspiration and ardor. The fencers fenced, the strong men lifted their heavy weights, the military companies drilled, the athletes tumbled and twisted, and climbed, and ran, and turned hand-springs; and the sportsmen and sharp-shooters shot, and shot, and shot, till their popping fairly peppered the general hum and buzz as if the place were undergoing a miniature bombardment.

And when nature needed refreshment or stimulus, one bottle of thin blue wine sufficed for the needs of any six of the participants; some of them, more ascetic, indeed, preferred lemonade, and shunned the wine-cup.

Before long Mr. Pentagon found himself in the very thick of it. He was introduced to everybody, and everybody made him welcome. As an American, he was regarded as a prime authority upon "*le sport,*" and he was called upon to act as umpire and referee in all manner of contests, most of them wholly strange to him. His umpiring must have been fearful and wonderful; but as the wildest of his decisions gave perfect satisfaction to everybody concerned, he was none the wiser. Then he got so interested that he began to take a hand in some of the milder sports, and with his hat on the back of his head, and his clerical necktie twisted around under one ear, he showed what an able-bodied American clergyman can do when he puts his whole mind on the noble game of ringtoss. And when Madame Perot came to tell him it was time to go home, she found him hand in hand with a string of little Perots and their playmates, capering clumsily but cheerfully to the tune of

> " Sur le pont d'Avignon,
> Tout le monde y danse, danse,
>   Sur le pont d'Avignon,
> Tout le monde y danse en rond."

As he approached the gate, weary but happy, he met the Doctor, who bore in his face a look more bright and more kindly (if that could be) than Mr. Pentagon had ever seen there before. The Doctor shook Mr. Pentagon warmly by the hand.

"My dear sir," he said, "I cannot tell you how pleased I am to see you here. I am afraid I should have expected to find you literally and figuratively on the other side of the fence. I have never yet been able to convince any one of your cloth of the necessity of allowing to the working people confined in great cities a chance for innocent and wholesome recreation on the one day that they can call their own. The workman in this country, and especially in New York, works harder and has fewer holidays than any workman in civilization. What with the climate and his three meals of meat a day, he has a tremendous head of steam on, and the standard of work which he makes for himself is such as no European employer would dare set up for his operatives. To condemn such a man to absolute idleness and inactivity one day in seven; to take his beer from him on that one day; to shut him out of

every place of innocent enjoyment in a city
that is tropically hot in summer, and cold as
Russia in winter, and that has only one narrow outlet to country walks, is cruel, my
dear sir—positively cruel. And when *you*
lend the sanction of your presence to Sunday
amusements, so innocent and helpful as these,
you are helping hundreds and thousands of
stunted lives, and doing more good than your
own eyes can see. Look around you! Is
there drunkenness here? Is there dissolute
conduct or disorder? Why, my dear sir,
these people are not only good citizens, but
devout members of their own church—it is
not yours or mine, but it is theirs. They have
been to early mass, and finished their de-
votions before you and I were out of bed,
and——"

The Doctor was growing eloquent, and
seemed to be but just started in his discourse.
Somehow the Reverend Mr. Pentagon, limp,
terrified, white of face, and weak as to his
knees, slipped away and out, through the big
gate on whose portals he saw for the first
time two huge signs on which he read but
two words "FÊTE" and "DIMANCHE."

.   .   .   .

The next day Mr. Pentagon went to New York, although he had neither supped nor slept the night before. He wanted to evade the Doctor's daily call, or at least to think things over with himself before he should meet that grave and thoughtful face. He was slowly and painfully walking down Fifth Avenue, his thoughts turned in upon himself, when he felt his hand grasped and warmly shaken. Lifting his eyes, he saw before him a face that gradually revealed itself to his memory as the face of the little vestryman, of the great church of his hopes, who had called upon him some months before to suggest the possibility of his coming to New York. The little man was beaming, and he flourished a newspaper.

"Good! good!" he said, shaking the clergyman's hand up and down, "you have done nobly, Mr. Pentagon! It was a daring thing, sir, very daring; but the very audacity of it has settled the business. The conservative element in our vestry is fairly frightened out of the field. Why, sir, Mr. McGlaisher, the leader of the Sabbatarian wing in our church, actually said that while he could not vote for you, he would not vote against you; and that

HE SAW FOR THE FIRST TIME TWO HUGE SIGNS

he could not help respecting a man who
had the courage of his convictions. You will
be called, sir, you will be called; as sure
as my name *ain't* McGlaisher."

And he bustled away, leaving the daily
paper in Mr. Pentagon's hands; and Mr.
Pentagon's weak and blinking eyes read:

NO BLUE LAWS FOR HIM!

THE REVEREND MR. PENTAGON ATTENDS A SUNDAY PICNIC.

AND DANCES WITH THE BABIES.

WILL ST. PHYLACTERY'S CALL HIM NOW?

.   .   .   .

That evening the Reverend Mr. Pentagon
made a confession to the Doctor—or rather
two confessions: one of error, and one of
conversion.

"But," said he, "will you tell me how it
was possible for me to make such an error?
The man certainly said *fifteen days*."

The Doctor's amused smile broadened.

"My dear sir," he said, "we Anglo-Saxons think we belong to the most logical race on the face of the earth, and yet the accurate little Frenchman can give us points three times out of four. With him a week is a *week*—seven days—with us it sometimes is, and sometimes is not. When you speak of something that happened 'a week ago this Monday,' you really speak of a period of eight days, or a week and the present Monday. The logical Frenchman does not even think of that space of time as a week; he calls it *huit jours*, in the same way. On the third Wednesday of your stay here, which happened, by the way, to be a saint's day in the Catholic Church, Monsieur Perot very rightly told you that you had been here fifteen days. But with your habit of counting '*exclusively*,' as we call our stupid fashion, you counted the days *done* and not the day you were in. You would not have done it if you had been calculating the date of payment of a note; it was simply illogical habit that counted for you. But you see," he concluded, with a little laugh, as he took up his hat, "you had been French for a fortnight."

"Ah, yes, I see," said the Reverend Mr. Pentagon.

And as he heard the Doctor close the front door behind him, he picked up his half-finished sermon "On the Duty of a Strict Observance of the Sabbath" and tore it into small pieces.

THE RED SILK HANDKER-
CHIEF

THE RED SILK HANDKER-
CHIEF

THE yellow afternoon sun came in through the long blank windows of the room wherein the Superior Court of the State of New York, Part II., Gillespie, Judge, was in session. The hour of adjournment was near at hand, a dozen court-loungers slouched on the hard benches in the attitudes of cramped carelessness which mark the familiar of the halls of justice. Beyond the rail sat a dozen lawyers and lawyers' clerks, and a dozen weary jurymen. Above the drowsy silence rose the nasal voice of the junior counsel for the defence, who in a high monotone, with his faint eyes fixed on the paper in his hand, was making something like a half-a-score of "requests to charge."

Nobody paid attention to him. Two law-yers' clerks whispered like mischievous schoolboys, hiding behind a pile of books that towered upon a table. Junior counsel for the plaintiff chewed his pencil and took advantage of his opportunity to familiarize himself with certain neglected passages of the New Code. The crier, like a half-dormant old spider, sat in his place and watched a boy who was fidgeting at the far end of the room, and who looked as though he wanted to whistle.

The jurymen might have been dream-men, vague creations of an autumn afternoon's doze. It was hard to connect them with a world of life and business. Yet, gazing closer, you might have seen that one looked as if he were thinking of his dinner, and another as if he were thinking of the lost love of his youth; and that the expression on the faces of the others ranged from the vacant to the inscrutable. The oldest juror, at the end of the second row, was sound asleep. Everyone in the court-room, except himself, knew it. No one cared.

Gillespie, J., was writing his acceptance of an invitation to a dinner set for that evening at Delmonico's. He was doing this in such a way that he appeared to be taking copious

and conscientious notes.   Long years on the
bench had whitened Judge Gillespie's hair,
and taught him how to do this.   His seem-
ing attentiveness much encouraged the counsel for the defence, whose high-pitched tone
rasped the air like the buzzing of a bee that
has found its way through the slats of the
blind into some darkened room, of a summer
noon, and that, as it seeks angrily for egress,
raises its shrill scandalized protest against
the idleness and the pleasant gloom.

"We r'quest y'r Honor t' charge : First, 't
forcible entry does not const'oot tresp'ss,
'nless intent's proved.   Thus, 'f a man rolls
down a bank——"

But the judge's thoughts were in the
private supper-room at Delmonico's.   He
had no interest in the sad fate of the hero
of the supposititious case, who had been
obliged, by a strange and ingenious combination of accidents, to make violent entrance,
incidentally damaging the persons and property of others, into the lands and tenements
of his neighbor.

And further away yet the droning lawyer
had set a-travelling the thoughts of Horace
Walpole, clerk for Messrs. Weeden, Snowden

& Gilfeather; for the young man sat with his elbows on the table, his head in his hands, a sad half-smile on his lips, and his brown eyes looking through vacancy to St. Lawrence County, New York.

He saw a great, shabby old house, shabby with the awful shabbiness of a sham grandeur laid bare by time and mocked by the pitiless weather. There was a great sham Grecian portico at one end; the white paint was well-nigh washed away, and the rain-streaked wooden pillars seemed to be weeping tears of penitence for having lied about themselves and pretended to be marble.

The battened walls were cracked and blistered. The Grecian temple on the hillock near looked much like a tomb, and not at all like a summer-house. The flower-garden was so rank and ragged, so overgrown with weed and vine, that it was spared the mortification of revealing its neglected maze, the wonder of the county in 1820. All was sham, save the decay. That was real; and by virtue of its decrepitude the old house seemed to protest against modern contempt, as though it said: " I have had my day. I was built when people thought this sort of

thing was the right sort of thing; when we
had our own little pseudo-classic renaissance
in America. I lie between the towns of
Aristotle and Sabine Farms. I am a gentleman's residence, and my name is Montevista.
I was built by a prominent citizen. You
need not laugh through your lattices, you
smug new Queen Anne cottage, down there
in the valley! What will become of you
when the falsehood is found out of your
imitation bricks and your tiled roof of
shingles, and your stained glass that is only
a sheet of transparent paper pasted on a
pane? You are a young sham; I am an old
one. Have some respect for age!"

Its age was the crowning glory of the
estate of Montevista. There was nothing
new on the place except a third mortgage.
Yet had Montevista villa put forth a juster
claim to respect, it would have said: "I have
had my day. Where all is desolate and
silent now, there was once light and life.
Along these halls and corridors, the arteries
of my being, pulsed a hot blood of joyous
humanity, fed with delicate fare, kindled
with generous wine. Every corner under
my roof was alive with love and hope and

ambition. Great men and dear women were here; and the host was great and the hostess was gracious among them all. The laughter of children thrilled my gaudily decked stucco. To-day an old man walks up and down my lonely drawing-rooms, with bent head, murmuring to himself odds and ends of tawdry old eloquence, wandering in a dead land of memory, waiting till Death shall take him by the hand and lead him out of his ruinous house, out of his ruinous life."

Death had indeed come between Horace and the creation of his spiritual vision. Never again should the old man walk, as to the boy's eyes he walked now, over the creaking floors, from where the Nine Muses simpered on the walls of the south parlor to where Homer and Plutarch, equally simpering, yet simpering with a difference—severely simpering—faced each other across the north room. Horace saw his father stalking on his accustomed round, a sad, familiar figure, tall and bent. The hands were clasped behind the back, the chin was bowed on the black stock; but every now and then the thin form drew itself straight, the fine, clean-shaven, aquiline face was raised, beaming with the

ghost of an old enthusiasm, and the long
right arm was lifted high in the air as he began, his sonorous tones a little tremulous in
spite of the restraint of old-time pomposity
and deliberation,

"Mr. Speaker, I rise;"—or, "If your
Honor please——"

The forlorn, helpless earnestness of this
mockery of life touched Horace's heart; and
yet he smiled to think how different were the
methods and manners of his father from
those of brother Hooper, whose requests still
droned up to the reverberating hollows of
the roof, and there were lost in a subdued
boom and snarl of echoes such as a court-
room only can beget.

Two generations ago, when the Honorable
Horace Kortlandt Walpole was the rising
young lawyer of the State; when he was
known as "the Golden-Mouthed Orator of St.
Lawrence County," he was in the habit of
assuming that he owned whatever court
he practised in; and, as a rule, he was right.
The most bullock-brained of country judges
deferred to the brilliant young master of law
and eloquence, and his "requests" were generally accepted as commands and obeyed

as such. Of course the great lawyer, for form's sake, threw a veil of humility over his deliverances; but even that he rent to shreds when the fire of his eloquence once got fairly aglow.

"May it please your Honor! Before your Honor exercises the sacred prerogative of your office—before your Honor performs the sacred duty which the State has given into your hands—before, with that lucid genius to which I bow my head, you direct the minds of these twelve good men and true in the path of strict judicial investigation, I ask your Honor to instruct them that they must bring to their deliberations that impartial justice which the laws of our beloved country—of which no abler exponent than your Honor has ever graced the bench—which the laws of our beloved country guarantee to the lowest as well as to the loftiest of her citizens—from the President in the Executive Mansion to the humble artisan at the forge—throughout this broad land, from the lagoons of Louisiana to where the snow-clad forests of Maine hurl defiance at the descendants of Tory refugees in the barren wastes of Nova Scotia——"

Horace remembered every word and every gesture of that speech. He recalled even the quick upward glance from under the shaggy eyebrows with which his father seemed to see again the smirking judge catching at the gross bait of flattery ; he knew the little pause which the speaker's memory had filled with the applause of an audience long since dispersed to various silent country grave-yards; and he wondered, pityingly, if it were possible that even in his father's prime that wretched allusion to old political hatreds had power to stir the fire of patriotism in the citizen's bosom.

"Poor old father!" said the boy to him-self. The voice which had for so many years been but an echo was stilled wholly now. Brief victory and long defeat were nothing now to the golden-mouthed orator.

"Shall I fail as he failed?" thought Horace: "No! I can't. Haven't I got *her* to work for?"

And then he drew out of his breast-pocket a red silk handkerchief and turned it over in his hand with a movement that concealed and caressed at the same time.

It was a very red handkerchief. It was

not vermilion, nor " cardinal," nor carmine, —a strange Oriental idealization of blood-red which lay well on the soft, fine, luxurious fabric. But it was an unmistakable, a shame-less, a barbaric red.

And as he looked at it, young Hitchcock, of Hitchcock & Van Rensselaer, came up behind him and leaned over his shoulder.

"Where did you get the handkerchief, Walpole?" he whispered; "you ought to hang that out for an auction flag, and sell out your cases."

Horace stuffed it back in his pocket.

" You'd be glad enough to buy some of them, if you got the show," he returned; but the opportunity for a prolonged contest of wit was cut short. The judge was folding his letter, and the nasal counsel, having finished his reading, stood gazing in doubt and trepi-dation at the bench, and asking himself why his Honor had not passed on each point as presented. He found out.

" Are you prepared to submit those requests in writing? " demanded Gillespie, J., sharply and suddenly. He knew well enough that that poor little nasal, nervous junior counsel would never have trusted himself to speak ten consecutive sentences in court without having every word on paper before him.

"Ye-yes," the counsel stammered, and handed up his careful manuscript.

"I will examine these to-night," said his Honor, and, apparently, he made an endorsement on the papers. He was really writing the address on the envelope of his letter. Then there was a stir, and a conversation between the judge and two or three lawyers, all at once, which was stopped when his Honor gave an Olympian nod to the clerk.

The crier arose.

"He' ye! he' ye! he' ye!" he shouted with perfunctory vigor. "Wah—wah—wah!" the high ceiling slapped back at him; and he declaimed, on one note, a brief address to "Awperns han bins" in that court, of which nothing was comprehensible save the words "Monday next at eleven o'clock." And then the court collectively rose, and individually put on hats for the most part of the sort called queer.

All the people were chattering in low voices; chairs were moved noisily, and the slumbering juror opened his weary eyes and troubled himself with an uncalled-for effort to look as though he had been awake all the time and didn't like the way things were going, at all. Horace got from the clerk the papers for which he had been waiting, and was passing out, when his Honor saw him and hailed him with an expressive grunt.

Gillespie, J., looked over his spectacles at Horace.

"Shall you see Judge Weeden at the office? Yes? Will you have the kindness to give him this—yes? If it's no trouble to you, of course."

Gillespie, J., was not over-careful of the feelings of lawyers' clerks, as a rule; but he had that decent disinclination to act *ultra præscriptum* which marks the attitude of the well-bred man toward his inferiors in office. He knew that he had no business to use Weeden, Snowden & Gilfeather's clerk as a messenger in his private correspondence.

Horace understood him, took the letter, and allowed himself a quiet smile when he reached the crowded corridor.

What mattered, he thought, as his brisk feet clattered down the wide stairs of the rotunda, the petty insolence of office *now?* He was Gillespie's messenger to-day; but had not his young powers already received recognition from a greater than Gillespie? If Judge Gillespie lived long enough he should put his gouty old legs under Judge Walpole's mahogany, and prose over his port —yes, he should have port, like the relic of mellow old days that he was—of the times "when your father-in-law and I, Walpole, were boys together."

Ah, there you have the spell of the Red Silk Handkerchief!

It was a wonderful tale to Horace; for he saw it in that wonderful light which shall shine on no man of us more than once in his life—on some of us not at all, Heaven help us!—but, in the telling, it is a simple tale:

"The Golden-Mouthed Orator of St. Lawrence" was at the height of his fame in that period of storm and stress which had the civil war for its climax. His misfortune was to be drawn into a contest for which he was not equipped, and in which he had little interest. His sphere of action was far from the battle-ground of the day. The intense localism that bounded his knowledge and his sympathies had but one break—he had tasted in his youth the extravagant hospitality of the South, and he held it in grateful remembrance. So it happened that he was a trimmer—a moderationist he called himself—a man who dealt in optimistic generalities, and who thought that if everybody—the slaves included—would only act temperately and reasonably, and view the matter from the stand-point of pure policy, the differences of South and North could be settled as easily as, through his own wise intervention, the old turnip-field feud of Farmer Oliver and Farmer Bunker had been wiped out of existence.

His admirers agreed with him, and they sent him to Congress to fill the unexpired short term of their representative, who had just died in Washington of what we now know as a malarial fever. It was not to be expected, perhaps, that the Honorable Mr. Walpole would succeed in putting a new face on the great political question in the course of his first term; but they all felt sure that his first speech would startle men who had never heard better than what Daniel Webster had had to offer them.

But the gods were against the Honorable Mr. Walpole. On the day set for his great effort there was what the theatrical people call a counter-attraction. Majah Pike had come up from Mizourah, sah, to cane that demn'd Yankee hound, Chahles Sumnah, sah, —yes, sah, to thrash him like a dawg, begad! And all Washington had turned out to see the performance, which was set down for a certain hour, in front of Mr. Sumner's door.

There was just a quorum when the golden-mouthed member began his great speech,— an inattentive, chattering crowd, that paid no attention to his rolling rhetoric and rococo grandiloquence. He told the empty seats what a great country this was, and how beautiful was a middle policy, and he illustrated this with a quotation from Homer, in the original Greek (a neat novelty : Latin was fashionable for parliamentary use in Webster's time), with, for the benefit of the uneducated, the well-known translation by the great Alexander Pope, commencing :

" To calm their passions with the words of Age,
  Slow from his seat arose the Pylian sage,
  Experienced Nestor, in Persuasion skilled,
  Words sweet as honey from his lips distilled."

When Nestor and Mr. Walpole closed, there was no quorum. The member from

New Jersey, who had engaged him in debate, was sleeping the sleep of honorable intoxication in his seat. Outside, all Washington was laughing and cursing. Majah Pike had not appeared.

It was the end of the golden-mouthed orator. His voice was never heard again in the House. His one speech was noticed only to be laughed at, and the news went home to his constituents. They showed that magnanimity which the poets tell us is an attribute of the bucolic character. They, so to speak, turned over the pieces of their broken idol with their cow-hide boots, and remarked that they had known it was clay, all along, and dern poor clay at that.

So the golden-mouthed went home, to try to make a ruined practice repair his ruined fortune; to give mortgages on his home to pay the debts his hospitality had incurred; to discuss with a few feeble old friends ways and means by which the war might have been averted; to beget a son of his old age, and to see the boy grow up in a new generation, with new ideas, new hopes, new ambitions, and a lifetime before him to make memories in.

They had little enough in common, but they came to be great friends as the boy grew older, for Horace inherited all his traits from the old man, except a certain stern energy which came from his silent, strong-hearted mother, and which his father saw with a sad joy.

Mr. Walpole sent his son to New York to study law in the office of Messrs. Weeden, Snowden & Gilfeather, who were a pushing young firm in 1850. Horace found it a very quiet and conservative old concern. Snowden and Gilfeather were dead; Weeden had been on the bench and had gone off the bench at the call of a "lucrative practice;" there were two new partners, whose names appeared only on the glass of the office door and in a corner of the letter-heads.

Horace read his law to some purpose. He became the managing clerk of Messrs. Weeden, Snowden & Gilfeather. This particular managing clerkship was one of unusual dignity and prospective profit. It meant, as it always does, great responsibility, little honor, and less pay. But the firm was so peculiarly constituted that the place was a fine stepping-stone for a bright and ambitious boy. One

10

of the new partners was a business man, who had put his money into the concern in 1860, and who knew and cared nothing about law. He kept the books and managed the money, and was beyond that only a name on the door and a terror to the office-boys. The other new partner was a young man who made a specialty of collecting debts. He could wring gold out of the stoniest and barrenest debtor; and there his usefulness ended. The general practice of the firm rested on the shoulders of Judge Weeden, who was old, lazy, and luxury-loving, and who, to tell the honest truth, shirked his duties. Such a state of affairs would have wrecked a younger house; but Weeden, Snowden & Gilfeather had a great name, and the consequences of his negligent feebleness had not yet descended upon Judge Weeden's head.

That they would, in a few years, that the Judge knew it, and that he was quite ready to lean on a strong young arm, Horace saw clearly.

That his own arm was growing in strength he also saw; and the Judge knew that, too. He was Judge Weeden's pet. All in the office recognized the fact. All, after reflection, concluded that it was a good thing that he was. New blood had to come into the firm sooner or later, and although it was not possible to watch the successful rise of this boy without a little natural envy and heart-burning, yet it was to be considered that Horace was one who would be honorable, just, and generous wherever fortune put him.

Horace was a gentleman. They all knew it. Barnes and Haskins, the business man and the champion collector, knew it down in the shallows of their vulgar little souls. Judge Weeden, who had some of that mysterious ichor of gentlehood in his wine-fed veins, knew it and rejoiced in it. And Horace—I can say for Horace that he never forgot it.

He was such a young prince of managing clerks that no one was surprised when he was sent down to Sand Hills, Long Island, to make preparations for the reorganization of the Great Breeze Hotel Company, and the transfer of the property known as the Breeze Hotel and Park to its new owners. The Breeze Hotel was a huge "Queen Anne" vagary which had, after the fashion of hotels, bankrupted its first owners, and was now going

into the hands of new people, who were likely
to make their fortunes out of it. The property had been in litigation for a year or so;
the mechanics' liens were numerous, and the
mechanics clamorous; and although the
business was not particularly complicated, it
needed careful and patient adjustment. Horace knew the case in every detail. He had
drudged over it all the winter, with no espe-
cial hope of personal advantage, but simply
because that was his way of working. He
went down in June to the mighty barracks,
and lived for a week in what would have been
an atmosphere of paint and carpet-dye had it
not been for the broad sea-wind that blew
through the five hundred open windows, and
swept rooms and corridors with salty freshness. The summering folk had not arrived
yet; there were only the new manager and
his six score of raw recruits of clerks and ser-
vants. But Horace felt the warm blood coming back to his cheeks, that the town had
somewhat paled, and he was quite content;
and every day he went down to the long,
lonely beach, and had a solitary swim, although the sharp water whipped his white
skin to a biting red. The sea takes a long

while to warm up to the summer, and is sullen about it.

He was to have returned to New York at the end of the week, and Haskins was to have taken his place; but it soon became evident to Weeden, Snowden & Gilfeather that the young man would attend to all that was to be done at Sand Hills quite as well as Mr. Haskins, or quite as well as Judge Weeden himself for that matter. He had to shoulder no great responsibility; the work was mostly of a purely clerical nature, vexatious enough, but simple. It had to be done on the spot, however; the original Breeze Hotel and Park Company was composed of Sand Hillers, and the builders were Sand Hillers, too, the better part of them. And there were titles to be searched; for the whole scheme was an ambitious splurge of Sand Hills pride and it had been undertaken and carried out in a reckless and foolish way. Horace knew all the wretched little details of the case, and so Horace was entrusted with duties such as do not often devolve upon a man of his years; and he took up his burden proudly, and with a glowing consciousness of his own strength.

Judge Weeden missed his active and intel-

ligent obedience in the daily routine of office
business; but the Judge thought that it was
just as well that Horace should not know the
fact. The young man's time would come soon
enough, and he would be none the worse for
serving his apprenticeship in modesty and
humility. The work entrusted to him was
an honor in itself. And then, there was no
reason why poor Walpole's boy shouldn't
have a sort of half-holiday out in the country
and enjoy his youth.

He was not recalled. The week stretched
out. He worked hard, found time to play,
hugged his quickened ambitions to his breast,
wrote hopeful letters to the mother at Mon-
tevesta, made a luxury of his loneliness, and
felt a bashful resentment when the " guests "
of the hotel began to pour in from the outside world.

For a day or two he fought shy of them.
But these first-comers were lonely, too, and
not so much in love with loneliness as he
thought he was, and very soon he became
one of them. He had found out all the walks
and drives; he knew the times of the tides;
he had made friends with the fishermen for a
league up and down the coast, and he had

amassed a store of valuable hints as to where
the first blue-fish might be expected to run.
Altogether he was a very desirable companion. Besides, that bright, fresh face of
his, and a certain look in it, made you friends
with him at once, especially if you happened
to be a little older, and to remember a look
of the sort, lost, lost forever, in a boy's look-
ing-glass.

So he was sought out, and he let himself
be found, and the gregarious instinct in him
waxed delightfully.

And then It came. Perhaps I should say
She came, but it is not the woman we love ;
it is our dream of her. Sweet and tender,
fair and good, she may be ; but let it be honor
enough for her that she has that glory about
her face which our love kindles to the halo
that lights many a man's life to the grave,
though the face beneath it be dead or
false.

I will not admit that it was only a pretty
girl from Philadelphia who came to Sand
Hills that first week in July. It was the rosy
goddess herself, dove-drawn across the sea,
in the warm path of the morning sun—
although the tremulous, old-fashioned hand-

writing on the hotel register only showed that the early train had brought—

"*Samuel Rittenhouse,*   *Philadelphia.*
"*Miss Rittenhouse,*   *do.*"

It was the Honorable Samuel Rittenhouse, ex-Chief Justice of Pennsylvania, the honored head of the Pennsylvania bar, and the legal representative of the Philadelphia contingent of the New Breeze Hotel and Park Company.

In the evening Horace called upon him in his rooms with a cumbersome stack of papers, and patiently waded through explanations and repetitions until Mr. Rittenhouse's testy courtesy—he had the nervous manner of age apprehensive of youthful irreverence—melted into a complacent and fatherly geniality. Then, when the long task was done and his young guest arose, he picked up the card that lay on the table and trained his glasses on it.

"'H. K. Walpole?'" he said. "Are you a New Yorker, sir?"

"From the north of the State," Horace told him.

"Indeed, indeed. Why, let me see—you

must be the son of my old friend Walpole—
of Otsego—wasn't it?" said the old gentleman, still tentatively.

"St. Lawrence, sir."

"Yes, St. Lawrence—of course, of course.
Why, I knew your father well, years ago, sir.
We were at college together."

"At Columbia?"

"Yes—yes. Why, bless me," Judge Rittenhouse went on, getting up to look at Horace, "you're the image of your poor father at
your age. A very brilliant man, sir, a very
able man. I did not see much of him after
we left college—I was a Pennsylvanian, and
he was from this State—but I have always
remembered your father with respect and regard, sir—a very able man. I think I heard
of his death some years ago."

"Three years ago," said Horace. His
voice fell somewhat. How little to this old
man of success was the poor, unnoticed death
of failure!

"Three years only!" repeated the Judge,
half apologetically. "Ah, people slip away
from each other in this world—slip away.
But I am glad to have met you, sir—very
much pleased indeed. Rosamond!"

For an hour the subdued creaking of a rocking-chair by the window had been playing a monotonously pleasant melody in Horace's ears. Now and then a coy wisp of bright hair, or the reflected ghost of it, had flashed into view in the extreme lower left-hand corner of a mirror opposite him. Once he had seen a bit of white brow under it, and from time to time the low flutter of turning magazine leaves had put in a brief second to the rocking-chair.

All this time Horace's brains had been among the papers on the table; but something else within him had been swaying to and fro with the rocking-chair, and giving a leap when the wisp of hair bobbed into sight.

Now the rocking-chair accompaniment ceased, and the curtained corner by the window yielded up its treasure, and Miss Rittenhouse came forward, with one hand brushing the wisp of hair back into place, as if she were on easy and familiar terms with it. Horace envied it.

"Rosamond," said the Judge, "this is Mr. Walpole, the son of my old friend Walpole. You have heard me speak of Mr. Walpole's father."

"Yes, papa," said the young lady, all but the corners of her mouth. And, oddly enough, Horace did not think of being saddened because this young woman had never heard of his father. Life was going on a new key, all of a sudden, with a hint of a melody to be unfolded that ran in very different cadences from the poor old tune of memory.

My heroine, over whose head some twenty summers had passed, was now in the luxuriant prime of her youthful beauty. Over a brow whiter than the driven snow fell clustering ringlets, whose hue—

That is the way the good old novelists and story tellers of the Neville and Beverley days would have set out to describe Miss Rittenhouse, had they known her. Fools and blind! As if anyone could describe—as if a poet, even, could more than hint at what a man sees in a woman's face when, seeing, he loves.

For a few moments the talkers were constrained, and the talk was meagre and desultory. Then the Judge, who had been rummaging around among the dust-heaps of his memory, suddenly recalled the fact that he had once, in stage-coach days, passed a night

at Montevista, and had been most hospitably
treated. He dragged this fact forth, pro-
fessed a lively remembrance of Mrs. Walpole — "a fine woman, sir, your mother; a
woman of many charms,"—asked after her
present health; and then, satisfied that he
had acquitted himself of his whole duty,
withdrew into the distant depths of his own
soul and fumbled over the papers Horace had
brought him, trying to familiarize himself
with them, as a commander might try to learn
the faces of his soldiers.

Then the two young people proceeded to
find the key together, and began a most har-
monious duet. Sand Hills was the theme.
Thus it was that they had to go out on the
balcony, where Miss Rittenhouse might gaze
into the brooding darkness over the sea, and
watch it wink a slow yellow eye with a humor-
ous alternation of sudden and brief red.
Thus, also, Horace had to explain how the
light-house was constructed. This moved
Miss Rittenhouse to scientific research. She
must see how it was done. Mr. Walpole
would be delighted to show her. Papa was
so much interested in those mechanical matters. Mr. Walpole had a team and light

wagon at his disposal, and would very much like to drive Miss Rittenhouse and her father over to the light-house. Miss Rittenhouse communicated this kind offer to her father. Her father saw what was expected of him, and dutifully acquiesced, like an obedient American father. Miss Rittenhouse had managed the Rittenhouse household and the head of the house of Rittenhouse ever since her mother's death.

Mr. Walpole really had a team at his disposal. He came from a country where people do not chase foxes, nor substitutes for foxes; but where they know and revere a good trotter. He had speeded many a friend's horse in training for the county fair. When he came to Sand Hills his soundness in the equine branch of a gentleman's education had attracted the attention of a horsey Sand-Hiller, who owned a showy team with a record of 2.37. This team was not to be trusted to the ordinary summer boarder on any terms; but the Sand-Hiller was thrifty and appreciative, and he lured Horace into hiring the turnout at a trifling rate, and thus captured every cent the boy had to spare, and got his horses judiciously exercised.

There was a showy light wagon to match the team, and the next day the light wagon, with Horace and the Rittenhouses in it, passed every carriage on the road to the light-house, where Miss Rittenhouse satisfied her scientific spirit with one glance at the lantern, after giving which glance she went outside and sat in the shade of the white tower with Horace, while the keeper showed the machinery to the Judge. Perhaps she went to the Judge afterward, and got him to explain it all to her.

Thus it began, and for two golden weeks thus it went on. The reorganized Breeze Hotel and Park Company met in business session on its own property, and Horace acted as a sort of honorary clerk to Judge Rittenhouse. The company, as a company, talked over work for a couple of hours each day. As a congregation of individuals, it ate and drank and smoked and played billiards and fished and slept the rest of the two dozen. Horace had his time pretty much to himself, or rather to Miss Rittenhouse, who monopolized it. He drove her to the village to match embroidery stuffs. He danced with her in the evenings, when two stolidly soulful Ger-

mans, one with a fiddle and the other with a
piano, made the vast dining-room ring and
hum with Suppé and Waldteufel, and this
was to the great and permanent improvement
of his waltzing. She taught him how to play
lawn-tennis—he was an old-fashioned boy
from the backwoods, and he thought that
croquet was still in existence, so she had to
teach him to play lawn-tennis—until he
learned to play much better than she could.
On the other hand, he was a fresh-water
swimmer of rare wind and wiriness, and a
young sea-god in the salt, as soon as he got
used to its pungent strength. So he taught
her to strike out beyond the surf-line, with
broad, breath-long sweeps, and there to float
and dive and make friends with the ocean.
Even he taught her to fold her white arms
behind her back, and swim with her feet. As
he glanced over his shoulder to watch her
following him, and to note the timorous, admiring crowd on the shore, she seemed a sea-
bred Venus of Milo in blue serge.

I have known men to be bored by such
matters. They made Horace happy. He
was happiest, perhaps, when he found out
that she was studying Latin. All the girls

in Philadelphia were studying Latin that
summer. They had had a little school
Latin, of course; but now their aims were
loftier. Miss Rittenhouse had brought with
her a Harkness's Virgil, an Anthon's dictionary, an old Bullion & Morris, and—yes, when
Horace asked her, she had brought an Inter-
linear; but she didn't mean to use it. They
rowed out to the buoy, and put the Inter-
linear in the sea. They sat on the sands
after the daily swim, and enthusiastically
labored, with many an unclassic excursus,
over P. V. Maronis Opera. Horace borrowed
some books of a small boy in the hotel, and
got up at five o'clock in the morning to run a
couple of hundred lines or so ahead of his
pupil, "getting out" a stint that would have
made him lead a revolt had any teacher im-
posed it upon his class a few years before—
for he was fresh enough from school to
have a little left of the little Latin that col-
leges give.

He wondered how it was that he had never
seen the poetry of the lines before. *Forsan
et hæc olim meminisse juvabit*—for perchance
it will joy us hereafter to remember these
things! He saw the wet and weary sailors

on the shore, hungrily eating, breathing hard
after their exertions; he heard the deep
cheerfulness of their leader's voice. The
wind blew toward him over the pine barrens,
as fresh as ever it blew past Dido's towers.
A whiff of briny joviality and adventurous
recklessness seemed to come from the page
on his knee. And to him, also, had not She
appeared who saw, hard by the sea, that
pious old buccaneer-Lothario, so much tossed
about on land and upon the deep?

This is what the moderns call a flirtation,
and I do not doubt that it was called a flirtation by the moderns around these two young
people. Somehow, though, they never got
themselves "talked about," not even by the
stranded nomads on the hotel verandas.
Perhaps this was because there was such a
joyous freshness and purity about both of
them that it touched the hearts of even the
slander-steeped old dragons who rocked all
day in the shade, and embroidered tidies and
talked ill of their neighbors. Perhaps it was
because they also had that about them which
the mean and vulgar mind always sneers at,
jeers at, affects to disbelieve in, always recog-
nizes and fears—the courage and power of

11

the finer strain. Envy in spit-curls and jealousy in a false front held their tongues, may be, because, though they knew that they, and even their male representatives, were safe from any violent retort, yet they recognized the superior force, and shrunk from it as the cur edges away from the quiescent whip.

There is a great difference, too, between the flirtations of the grandfatherless and the flirtations of the grandfathered. I wish you to understand that Mr. Walpole and Miss Rittenhouse did not *sprawl* through their flirtation, nor fall into that slipshod familiarity which takes all the delicate beauty of dignity and mutual respect out of such a friendship. Horace did not bow to the horizontal, and Miss Rittenhouse did not make a cheesecake with her skirts when he held open the door for her to pass through; but the bond of courtesy between them was no less sweetly gracious on her side, no less finely reverential on his, than the taste of their grandparents' day would have exacted—no less earnest, I think, that it was a little easier than puff and periwig might have made it.

Yet I also think, whatever was the reason that made the dragons let them alone, that a simple mother of the plain, old-fashioned style is better for a girl of Miss Rosamond Rittenhouse's age than any such precarious immunity from annoyance.

Ah, the holiday was short! The summons soon came for Horace. They went to the old church together for the second and last time, and he stood beside her, and they held the hymn-book between them.

Horace could not rid himself of the idea that they had stood thus through every Sunday of a glorious summer. The week before he had sung with her. He had a boyish baritone in him, one of those which may be somewhat extravagantly characterized as consisting wholly of middle register. It was a good voice for the campus, and, combined with that startling clearness of utterance which young collegians acquire, had been very effective in the little church. But to-day he had no heart to sing "Byefield" and "Pleyel;" he would rather stand beside her and feel his heart vibrate to the deep lower notes of her tender contralto, and his soul rise with the higher tones that soared upward from her pure young breast. And all the while he was making that act of devotion which—"uttered or unexpressed"—is, indeed, all the worship earth has ever known.

Once she looked up at him as if she asked, "Why don't you sing?" But her eyes fell quickly, he thought with a shade of displeasure in them at something they had seen in his. Yet as he watched her bent head, the cheek near him warmed with a slow, soft blush. He may only have fancied that her clear voice quivered a little with a tremulo not written in the notes at the top of the page.

And now the last day came. When the work-a-day world thrust its rough shoulder into Arcadia, and the hours of the idyl were numbered, they set to talking of it as though the two weeks that they had known each other were some sort of epitomized summer. Of course they were to meet again, in New York or in Philadelphia; and of course there were many days of summer in store for Miss Rittenhouse at Sand Hills, at Newport, and at Mount Desert; but Horace's brief season was closed, and somehow she seemed to fall readily into his way of looking upon it as a golden period of special and important value, their joint and exclusive property—something set apart from all the rest of her holiday, where there would be other men and other good times and no Horace.

It was done with much banter and merriment; but through it all Horace listened for delicate undertones that should echo to his ear the earnestness which sometimes rang irrepressibly in his own speech. In that marvellous instrument, a woman's voice, there are strange and fine possibilities of sound that may be the messengers of the subtlest intelligence or the sweet falterings of imperfect control. So Horace, with love to construe for him, did not suffer too cruelly from disappointment.

On the afternoon of that last day they sat upon the beach and saw the smoke of Dido's funeral pile go up, and they closed the dog's-eared Virgil, and, looking seaward, watched the black clouds from a coaling steamer mar the blinding blue where sea and sky blent at the horizon, watched it grow dull and faint, and fade away, and the illumined turquoise reassert itself.

Then he was for a farewell walk, and she, with that bright acquiescence with which a young girl can make companionship almost perfect, if she will, accepted it as an inspira-

tion, and they set out. They visited together the fishermen's houses, where Horace
bade good-by to mighty fisted friends, who
stuck their thumbs inside their waistbands
and hitched their trousers half way up to
their blue-shirted arms, and said to him,
"You come up here in Orgust, Mr. Walpole
—say 'bout the fus't' the third week 'n Orgust, 'n' we'll give yer some bloo-fishin' 't y'
won't need t' lie about, neither." They all
liked him, and heartily.

Old Rufe, the gruff hermit of the fishers,
who lived a half-mile beyond the settlement,
flicked his shuttle through the net he was
mending, and did not look up as Horace
spoke to him.

"Goin'?" he said; "waal, we've all gotter
go some time or uther. The' ain't no real
perma-nen-cy on this uth. Goin'? Waal,
I'm "—he paused, and weighed the shuttle in
his hand as though to aid him in balancing
some important mental process. "Sho! I'm
derned 'f I ain't sorry. Squall comin' up, an'
don't y' make no mistake," he hurried on, not
to be further committed to unguarded expression; "better look sharp, or y'll git a
wettin'."

A little puff of gray cloud, scurrying along in the southeast, had spread over half the sky, and now came a strong, eddying wind. A big raindrop made a dark spot on the sand before them; another fell on Miss Rittenhouse's cheek, and then, with a vicious, uncertain patter, the rain began to come down.

"We'll have to run for Poinsett's," said Horace, and stretched out his hand. She took it, and they ran.

Poinsett's was just ahead—a white house on a lift of land, close back of the shore line, with a long garden stretching down in front, and two or three poplar trees. The wind was turning up the pale undersides of grass-blade and flower leaf, and whipping the shivering poplars silver white. Cap'n Poinsett, late of Gloucester, Massachusetts, was tacking down the path in his pea-jacket, with his brass telescope tucked under his arm. He was making for the little white summer-house that overhung the shore; but he stopped to admire the two young people dashing up the slope toward him, for the girl ran with a splendid free stride that kept her well abreast of Horace's athletic lope.

"Come in," he said, opening the gate.

and smiling on the two young faces, flushed and wet; "come right in out o' the rain. Be'n runnin', ain't ye? Go right int' the house. Mother!" he called, "here's Mr. Walpole 'n' his young lady. You'll hev to ex-cuse me; I'm a-goin' down t' my observatory. I carn't foller the sea no longer myself, but I can look at them that dooz. There's my old woman—go right in."

He waddled off, leaving both of them redder than their run accounted for, and Mrs. Poinsett met them at the door, her arms folded in her apron.

"Walk right in," she greeted them; "the cap'n he mus' always go down t' his observatory, 's he calls it, 'n' gape through thet old telescope of hisn, fust thing the 's a squall —jus' 's if he thought he was skipper of all Long Island. But you come right int' the settin'-room 'n' make yourselves to home. Dear me suz! 'f I'd 'a' thought I'd 'a' had company I'd 'a' tidied things up. I'm jus' 's busy, *as* busy, gettin' supper ready; but don't you mind *me*—jus' you make yourselves to home," and she drifted chattering away, and they heard her in the distant kitchen amiably nagging the hired girl.

It was an old-time, low-ceiled room, neat with New England neatness. The windows had many pains of green flint glass, through which they saw the darkening storm swirl over the ocean and ravage the flower-beds near by.

And when they had made an end of watching Cap'n Poinsett in his little summer-house, shifting his long glass to follow each scudding sail far out in the darkness; and when they had looked at the relics of Cap'n Poinsett's voyages to the Orient and the Arctic, and at the cigar-boxes plastered with little shells, and at the wax fruit, and at the family trousers and bonnets in the album, there was nothing left but that Miss Rittenhouse should sit down at the old piano, bought for Amanda Jane in the last year of the war, and bring forth rusty melody from the yellowed keys.

"What a lovely voice she has!" thought Horace as she sang. No doubt he was right. I would take his word against that of a professor of music, who would have told you that it was a nice voice for a girl, and that the young woman had more natural dramatic expression than technical training.

They fished out Amanda Jane's music-books, and went through " Juanita," and the " Evergreen Waltz," and "Beautiful Isle of the Sea ;" and, finding a lot of war-songs, severally and jointly announced their determination to invade Dixie Land, and to annihilate Rebel Hordes ; and adjured each other to remember Sumter and Baltimore, and many other matters that could have made but slight impression on their young minds twenty odd years before. Mrs. Poinsett, in the kitchen, stopped nagging her aid, and thought of young John Tarbox Poinsett's name on a great sheet of paper in the Gloucester post-office, one morning at the end of April, 1862, when the news came that Farragut had passed the forts.

The squall was going over, much as it had come, only no one paid attention to its movements now, for the sun was out, trying to straighten up the crushed grass and flowers, and to brighten the hurrying waves, and to soothe the rustling agitation of the poplars.

They must have one more song. Miss Rittenhouse chose " Jeannette and Jeannot," and when she looked back at him with

a delicious coy mischief in her eyes, and
sang,—

> " There is no one left to love me now,
>   And you too may forget "—

Horace felt something flaming in his cheeks
and choking in his breast, and it was hard
for him to keep from snatching those hands
from the keys and telling her she knew better.

But he was man enough not to. He con-
trolled himself, and made himself very pleasant to Mrs. Poinsett about not staying to
supper, and they set out for the hotel.

The air was cool and damp after the
rain.

" You've been singing," said Horace, " and
you will catch cold in this air, and lose
your voice. You must tie this handkerchief
around your throat."

She took his blue silk handkerchief and
tied it around her throat, and wore it until
just as they were turning away from the
shore, when she took it off to return to him ;
and the last gust of wind that blew that afternoon whisked it out of her hand, and sent it
whirling a hundred yards out to sea.

"Now, don't say a word," said Horace; "it isn't of the slightest consequence."

But he looked very gloomy over it. He had made up his mind that that silk handkerchief should be the silk handkerchief of all the world to him, from that time on.

.   .   .   .

It was one month later that Mr. H. K. Walpole received, in care of Messrs. Weeden, Snowden & Gilfeather, an envelope postmarked Newport, containing a red silk handkerchief. His initials were neatly—nay, beautifully, exquisitely—stitched in one corner. But there was absolutely nothing about the package to show who sent it, and Horace sorrowed over this. Not that he was in any doubt; but he felt that it meant to say that he must not acknowledge it; and, loyally, he did not.

And he soon got over that grief. The lost handkerchief, whose origin was base and common, like other handkerchiefs, and whose sanctity was purely accidental—what was it to *this* handkerchief, worked by her for him?

This became the outward and visible sign of the inward and spiritual grace that had changed the boy's whole life. Before this he had had purposes and ambitions. He had meant to take care of his mother, to do well in the world, and to restore, if he could, the honor and glory of the home his father had left him. Here were duty, selfishness, and an innocent vanity. But now he had an end in life, so high that the very seeking of it was a religion. Every thought of self was flooded out of him, and what he sought he sought in a purer and nobler spirit than ever before.

Is it not strange? A couple of weeks at the sea-side, a few evenings under the brooding darkness of hotel verandas, the going to and fro of a girl with a sweet face, and this ineradicable change is made in the mind of a man who has forty or fifty years before him wherein to fight the world, to find his place, to become a factor for good or evil.

And here we have Horace, with his heart full of love and his head full of dreams, mooning over a silk handkerchief, in open court.

Not that he often took such chances. The daws of humor peck at the heart worn on the sleeve; and quite rightly, for that is no place for a heart. But in the privacy of his modest lodging-house room he took the handkerchief out, and spread it before him, and looked at it, and kissed it sometimes, I suppose—it seems ungentle to pry thus into the sacredness of a boy's love—and, certainly, kept it in sight, working, studying, or thinking.

With all this, the handkerchief became somewhat rumpled, and at last Horace felt that it must be brought back to the condition of neatness in which he first knew it. So, on a Tuesday, he descended to the kitchen of his lodging - house, and asked for a flat - iron. His good landlady, at the head of an industrious, plump - armed Irish brigade, all vigorously smoothing out towels, stared at him in surprise.

"If there's anything you want ironed, Mr. Walpole, bring it down here, and I'll be *more'n* glad to iron it for you."

Horace grew red, and found his voice going entirely out of his control, as he tried to explain that it wasn't for that—it wasn't for ironing clothes — he was sure nobody could do it but himself.

"Do you want it hot or cold?" asked Mrs. Wilkins, puzzled.

"Cold!" said Horace desperately. And

he got it cold, and had to heat it at his own fire to perform his labor of love.

That was of a piece with many things he did. Of a piece, for instance, with his looking in at the milliners' windows and trying to think which bonnet would best become her — and then taking himself severely to task for dreaming that she would wear a ready - made bonnet. Of a piece with his buying two seats for the theatre, and going alone and fancying her next him, and glancing furtively at the empty place at the points where he thought she would be amused, or pleased, or moved.

What a fool he was! Yes, my friend, and so are you and I. And remember that this boy's foolishness did not keep him tossing, stark awake, through ghastly nights; did not start him up in the morning with a hot throat and an unrested brain; did not send him down to his day's work with the haunting, clutching, lurking fear that springs forward at every stroke of the clock, at every opening of the door. Perhaps you and I have known folly worse than his.

Through all the winter — the red handkerchief cheered the hideous first Monday in

October, and the Christmas holidays, when
business kept him from going home to
Montevista — he heard little or nothing of
her.   His friends in the city, or rather his
father's friends, were all ingrained New
Yorkers, dating from the provincial period,
who knew not Philadelphia ; and it was only
from an occasional newspaper paragraph that
he learned that Judge Rittenhouse and his
daughter were travelling through the South,
for the Judge's health.   Of course, he had a
standing invitation to call on them whenever,
he should find himself in Philadelphia ; but
they never came nearer Philadelphia than
Washington, and so he never found himself
in Philadelphia.   He was not so sorry for
this as you might think a lover should be.
He knew that, with a little patience, he might
present himself to Judge Rittenhouse as
something more than a lawyer's managing
clerk.

For, meanwhile, good news had come from
home, and things were going well with him.
Mineral springs had been discovered at
Aristotle—mineral springs may be discovered
anywhere in north New York, if you only
try ; though it is sometimes difficult to fit

them with the proper Indian legends. The
name of the town had been changed to
Avoca, and there was already an Avoca
Improvement Company, building a big hotel,
advertising right and left, and prophesying
that the day of Saratoga and Sharon and
Richfield was ended. So the barrens between
Montevista and Aristotle, skirting the railroad,
suddenly took on a value. Hitherto they had
been unsalable, except for taxes. For the
most part they were an adjunct of the estate
of Montevista ; and in February Horace went
up to St. Lawrence County and began the
series of sales that was to realize his father's
most hopeless dream, and clear Montevista of
all incumbrances.

How pat it all came, he thought, as, on his
return trip, the train carried him past the
little old station, with its glaring new sign,
AVOCA, just beyond the broad stretch of
"Squire Walpole's bad land," now sprouting
with the surveyors' stakes. After all was
paid off on the old home, there would be
enough left to enable him to buy out
Haskins, who had openly expressed his
desire to get into a "live firm," and who was
willing to part with his interest for a reason-

12

able sum down, backed up by a succession of easy instalments. And Judge Weeden had intimated, as clearly as dignity would permit, his anxiety that Horace should seize the opportunity.

. . . .

Winter was still on the Jersey flats on the last day of March; but Horace, waiting at a little "flag station," found the air full of crude prophecies of spring. He had been searching titles all day, in a close and gloomy little town-hall, and he was glad to be out-of-doors again, and to think that he should be back in New York by dinner time, for it was past five o'clock.

But a talk with the station-master made the prospect less bright. No train would stop there until seven.

Was there no other way of getting home? The lonely guardian of the Gothic shanty thought it over, and found that there was a way. He talked of the trains as though they were whimsical creatures under his charge.

"The's a freight coming down right now," he said, meditatively, "but I can't do nothin' with her. She gotter get along mighty lively to keep ahead of the Express from Philadel-

phia till she gets to the junction and goes on
a siding till the Express goes past. And as
to the Express—why, I couldn't no more flag
her than if she was a cyclone. But I tell you
what you do. You walk right down to the
junction—'bout a mile 'n' a half down—and
see if you can't do something with number
ninety-seven on the other road. You see, she
goes on to New York on our tracks, and she
mostly 's in the habit of waiting at the junction
'bout—say five to seven minutes, to give that
Express from Philadelphia a fair start. That
Express has it pretty much her own way on
this road, for a fact. You go down to the
junction — walk right down the line — and
you 'll get ninety-seven—there ain't no kind
of doubt about it. You can't see the junction; but it's just half a mile beyont that
curve down there."

So there was nothing to be done but to
walk to the junction. The railroad ran a
straight, steadily descending mile on the top
of a high embankment, and then suddenly
turned out of sight around a ragged elevation.
Horace buttoned his light overcoat, and
tramped down the cinder-path between the
tracks.

Yes, spring was coming. The setting sun beamed a soft, hopeful red over the shoulder of the ragged elevation ; light, drifting mists rose from the marsh land below him, and the last low rays struck a vapory opal through them. There was a warm, almost prismatic purple hanging over the outlines of the hills and woods far to the east. The damp air, even, had a certain languid warmth in it ; and though there was snow in the little hollows at the foot of the embankment, and bits of thin whitish ice were in the swampy pools, it was clear enough to Horace that spring was at hand. Spring—and then summer; and, by the sea or in the mountains, the junior partner of the house of Weeden, Snowden & Gilfeather might hope to meet once more with Judge Rittenhouse's daughter.

The noise of the freight train, far up the track behind him, disturbed Horace's springtime revery. A forethought of rocking gravelcars scattering the overplus of their load by the way, and of reeking oil-tanks, filling the air with petroleum, sent him down the embankment to wait until the way was once more clear.

The freight train went by and above him

with a long-drawn roar and clatter, and with
a sudden fierce crash, and the shriek of iron
upon iron, at the end, and the last truck of the
last car came down the embankment, tearing
a gully behind it, and ploughed a grave for
itself in the marsh ten yards ahead of him.

And, looking up, he saw a twisted rail raising its head like a shining serpent above the
dim line of the embankment. A furious rush
took Horace up the slope. A quarter of a
mile below him the freight train was slipping
around the curve. The fallen end of the last
car was beating and tearing the ties. He heard
the shrill shriek of the brakes and the frightened whistle of the locomotive. But the
grade was steep, and it was hard to stop.
And if they did stop they were half a mile
from the junction—half a mile from their only
chance of warning the Express.

Horace heard in his ears the station-
master's words: "She's gotter get along
mighty lively to keep ahead of the Express
from Philadelphia."

"Mighty lively — mighty lively" — the
words rang through his brain to the time
of thundering car-wheels.

He knew where he stood. He had made

three-quarters of the straight mile. He was three-quarters of a mile, then, from the little station. His overcoat was off in half a second. Many a time had he stripped, with that familiar movement, to trunks and sleeveless shirt, to run his mile or his half-mile; but never had such a thirteen hundred yards lain before him, up such a track, to be run for such an end.

The sweat was on his forehead before his right foot passed his left.

His young muscles strove and stretched. His feet struck the soft, unstable path of cinders with strong, regular blows. His tense forearms strained upward from his sides. Under his chest, thrown outward from his shoulders, was a constricting line of pain. His wet face burnt. There was a fire in his temples, and at every breath of his swelling nostrils something throbbed behind his eyes. The eyes saw nothing but a dancing dazzle of tracks and ties, through a burning blindness. And his feet beat, beat, beat, till the shifting cinders seemed afire under him.

That is what this human machine was doing, going at this extreme pressure; every muscle, every breath, every drop of blood alive with the pain of this intense stress. Looking at it you would have said, " A fleet, light-limbed young man, with a stride like a deer, throwing the yards under him in fine style." All we know about the running other folks are making in this world!

Half-way up the track Horace stopped short, panting hard, his heart beating like a crazy drum, a nervous shiver on him. Up the track there was a dull whirr, and he saw the engine of the express-train slipping down on him—past the station already.

The white mists from the marshes had risen up over the embankment. The last rays of the sunset shot through them, brilliant and blinding. Horace could see the engine ; but would the engineer see him, waving his hands in futile gestures, in time to stop on that slippery, sharp grade ? And of what use would be his choking voice when the dull whirr should turn into a roar ? For a moment, in his hopeless disappointment, Horace felt like throwing himself in the path of the train, like a wasted thing that had no right to live, after so great a failure.

As will happen to those who are stunned

by a great blow, his mind ran back mechanically to the things nearest his heart, and in a flash he went through the two weeks of his life. And then, before the thought had time to form itself, he had brought a red silk handkerchief from his breast, and was waving it with both hands, a fiery crimson in the opal mist.

Seen. The whistle shrieked; there was a groan and a creak of brakes, the thunder of the train resolved itself into various rattling noises, the engine slipped slowly by him, and slowed down, and he stood by the platform of the last car as the express stopped.

There was a crowd around Horace in an instant. His head was whirling, but in a dull way he said what he had to say. An officious passenger, who would have explained it all to the conductor if the conductor had waited, took the deliverer in his arms—for the boy was near fainting—and enlightened the passengers who flocked around.

Horace hung in his embrace, too deadly weak even to accept the offer of one of the dozen flasks that were thrust at him. Nothing was very clear in his mind; as far as he could make out, his most distinct impression was of a broad, flat beach, a blue sea and a blue sky, a black steamer making a black trail of smoke across them, and a voice soft as an angel's reading Latin close by him. Then he opened his eyes and saw the woman of the voice standing in front of him.

"Oh, Richard," he heard her say, "it's Mr. Walpole!"

Horace struggled to his feet. She took his hand in both of hers and drew closer to him; the crowd falling back a little, seeing that they were friends.

"What can I ever say to thank you?" she said. "You have saved our lives. It's not so much for myself, but"—she blushed faintly, and Horace felt her hands tremble on his—"Richard—my husband—we were married to-day, you know—and——"

Something heavy and black came between Horace and life for a few minutes. When it passed away he straightened himself up out of the arms of the officious passenger and stared about him, mind and memory coming back to him. The people around looked at him oddly. A brakeman brought him his overcoat, and he stood unresistingly while it

was slipped on him. Then he turned away
and started down the embankment.

"Hold on!" cried the officious passenger ex-
citedly ; "we're getting up a testimonial ——"

Horace never heard it. How he found his
way he never cared to recall ; but the gas
was dim in the city streets, and the fire was
out in his little lodging-house room when he
came home ; and his narrow white bed knows
all that I cannot tell of his tears and his
broken dreams.

.   .   .   .

"Walpole," said Judge Weeden, as he
stood between the yawning doors of the office safe, one morning in June, "I observe
that you have a private package here. Why
do you not use the drawer of our—our late
associate, Mr. Haskins? It is yours now,
you know. I'll put your package in it." He
poised the heavily sealed envelope in his
hand. "Very odd *feeling* package, Walpole.
Remarkably soft!" he said. "Well, bless
me, it's none of my business, of course.
Horace, how much you look like your
father!"

OUR AROMATIC UNCLE

OUR AROMATIC UNCLE

IT is always with a feeling of personal
tenderness and regret that I recall his
story, although it began long before I was
born, and must have ended shortly after that
important date, and although I myself never
laid eyes on the personage of whom my wife
and I always speak as " The Aromatic
Uncle."

The story begins so long ago, indeed, that
I can tell it only as a tradition of my wife's
family. It goes back to the days when Boston was so frankly provincial a town that
one of its leading citizens, a man of eminent
position and ancient family, remarked to a
young kinsman whom he was entertaining at
his hospitable board, by way of pleasing
and profitable discourse: "Nephew, it may
interest you to know that it is Mr. Everett
who has the *other* hindquarter of this lamb."
This simple tale I will vouch for, for I got it

from the lips of the nephew, who has been my uncle for so many years that I know him to be a trustworthy authority.

In those days which seem so far away— and yet the space between them and us is spanned by a lifetime of three-score years and ten—life was simpler in all its details; yet such towns as Boston, already old, had well-established local customs which varied not at all from year to year; many of which lingered in later phases of urban growth. In Boston, or at least in that part of Boston where my wife's family dwelt, it was the invariable custom for the head of the family to go to market in the early morning with his wife's list of the day's needs. When the list was filled, the articles were placed in a basket; and the baskets thus filled were systematically deposited by the market-boys at the back-door of the house to which they were consigned. Then the house-keeper came to the back-door at her convenience, and took the basket in. Exposed as this position must have been, such a thing as a theft of the day's edibles was unknown, and the first authentic account of any illegitimate handling of the baskets brings me to the introduction of my wife's uncle.

IT WAS ON A SUMMER MORNING

It was on a summer morning, as far as I
can find out, that a little butcher-boy—a very
little butcher-boy to be driving so big a cart
—stopped in the rear of two houses that
stood close together in a suburban street.
One of these houses belonged to my wife's
father, who was, from all I can gather, a very
pompous, severe, and generally objectionable
old gentleman; a Judge, and a very considerable dignitary, who apparently devoted all his
leisure to making life miserable for his family.
The other was owned by a comparatively poor
and unimportant man, who did a shipping
business in a small way. He had bought it
during a period of temporary affluence, and it
hung on his hands like a white elephant. He
could not sell it, and it was turning his hair
gray to pay the taxes on it. On this particular morning he had got up at four o'clock to
go down to the wharves to see if a certain
ship in which he was interested had arrived.
It was due and overdue, and its arrival would
settle the question of his domestic comfort
for the whole year; for if it failed to appear,
or came home with an empty bottom, his fate
would be hard indeed; but if it brought him
money or marketable goods from its long

Oriental trip, he might take heart of grace
and look forward to better times.

When the butcher's boy stopped at the
house of my wife's father, he set down at the
back-door a basket containing fish, a big joint
of roast beef, and a generous load of fruit and
vegetables, including some fine, fat oranges.
At the other door he left a rather unpromis-
ing-looking lump of steak and a half-peck of
potatoes, not of the first quality. When he
had deposited these two burdens he ran back
and started his cart up the road.

But he looked back as he did so, and he
saw a sight familiar to him, and saw the com-
mission of a deed entirely unfamiliar. A
handsome young boy of about his own age
stepped out of the back-door of my wife's
father's house and looked carelessly around
him. He was one of the boys who compel
the admiration of all other boys — strong,
sturdy, and a trifle arrogant.

He had long ago compelled the admiration
of the little butcher-boy. They had been
playmates together at the public school, and
although the Judge's son looked down from
an infinite height upon his poor little com-
rade, the butcher-boy worshipped him with

the deepest and most fervent adoration. He
had for him the admiring reverence which the
boy who can't lick anybody has for the boy
who can lick everybody. He was a superior
being, a pattern, a model; an ideal never to
be achieved, but perhaps in a crude, humble
way to be imitated. And there is no hero-
worship in the world like a boy's worship of
a boy-hero.

The sight of this fortunate and adorable
youth was familiar enough to the butcher-
boy, but the thing he did startled and shocked
that poor little workingman almost as much
as if his idol had committed a capital crime
right before his very eyes. For the Judge's
son suddenly let a look into his face that
meant mischief, glanced around him to see
whether anybody was observing him or not,
and, failing to notice the butcher-boy, quickly
and dexterously changed the two baskets.
Then he went back into the house and shut
the door on himself.

The butcher-boy reined up his horse and
jumped from his cart. His first impulse, of
course, was to undo the shocking iniquity
which the object of his admiration had committed. But before he had walked back a

13

dozen yards, it struck him that he was taking
a great liberty in spoiling the other boy's
joke. It was wrong, of course, he knew it;
but was it for him to rebuke the wrong-doing
of such an exalted personage? If the Judge's
son came out again, he would see that his
joke had miscarried, and then he would be
displeased. And to the butcher-boy it did
not seem right in the nature of things that
anything should displease the Judge's son.
Three times he went hesitatingly backward
and forward, trying to make up his mind, and
then he made it up. The king could do no
wrong. Of course he himself was doing
wrong in not putting the baskets back where
they belonged; but then he reflected, he took
that sin on his own humble conscience, and
in some measure took it off the conscience of
the Judge's son—if, indeed, it troubled that
lightsome conscience at all. And, of course,
too, he knew that, being an apprentice, he
would be whipped for it when the substitu-
tion was discovered. But he didn't mind
being whipped for the boy he worshipped.
So he drove out along the road; and the wife
of the poor shipping-merchant, coming to the
back-door, and finding the basket full of

good things, and noticing especially the
beautiful China oranges, naturally concluded
that her husband's ship had come in, and
that he had provided his family with a rare
treat. And the Judge, when he came home
to dinner, and Mrs. Judge introduced him to
the rump-steak and potatoes—but I do not
wish to make this story any more pathetic
than is necessary.

.   .   .   .

A few months after this episode, perhaps
indirectly in consequence of it—I have never
been able to find out exactly—the Judge's
son, my wife's uncle, ran away to sea, and for
many years his recklessness, his strength,
and his good looks were only traditions in
the family, but traditions which he himself
kept alive by remembrances than which none
could have been more effective.

At first he wrote but seldom, later on more
regularly, but his letters—I have seen many
of them—were the most uncommunicative
documents that I ever saw in my life. His
wanderings took him to many strange places
on the other side of the globe, but he never
wrote of what he saw or did. His family

gleaned from them that his health was good,
that the weather was such-and-such, and that
he wished to have his love, duty, and respects
conveyed to his various relatives. In fact,
the first positive bit of personal intelligence
that they received from him was five years
after his departure, when he wrote them from
a Chinese port on letter-paper whose heading
showed that he was a member of a com-
mercial firm. The letter itself made no
mention of the fact. As the years passed on,
however, the letters came more regularly and
they told less about the weather, and were
slightly—very slightly—more expressive of a
kind regard for his relatives. But at the
best they were cramped by the formality of
his day and generation, and we of to-day
would have called them cold and perfunctory.

But the practical assurances that he gave
of his undiminished—nay, his steadily in-
creasing—affection for the people at home,
were of a most satisfying character, for they
were convincing proof not only of his love
but of his material prosperity. Almost from
his first time of writing he began to send
gifts to all the members of the family. At
first these were mere trifles, little curios of

travel such as he was able to purchase out of
a seaman's scanty wages; but as the years
went on they grew richer and richer, till the
munificence of the runaway son became the
pride of the whole family.

The old house that had been in the suburbs of Boston was fairly in the heart of the
city when I first made its acquaintance, and
one of the famous houses of the town. And
it was no wonder it was famous, for such
a collection of Oriental furniture, bric-à-brac,
and objects of art never was seen outside of a
museum. There were ebony cabinets, book-
cases, tables, and couches wonderfully carved
and inlaid with mother-of-pearl. There were
beautiful things in bronze and jade and ivory.
There were all sorts of strange rugs and
curtains and portières. As to the china-ware
and the vases, no house was ever so stocked;
and as for such trifles as shawls and fans and
silk handkerchiefs, why such things were sent
not singly but by dozens.

No one could forget his first entrance into
that house. The great drawing-room was
darkened by heavy curtains, and at first you
had only a dim vision of the strange and
graceful shapes of its curious furnishing.

But you could not but be instantly conscious of the delicate perfume that pervaded the apartment, and, for the matter of that, the whole house. It was a combination of all the delightful Eastern smells—not sandal-wood only, nor teak, nor couscous, but all these odors and a hundred others blent in one. Yet it was not heavy nor overpowering, but delightfully faint and sweet, diffused through those ample rooms. There was good reason, indeed, for the children of the generation to which my wife belonged to speak of the generous relative whom they had never seen as " Our Aromatic Uncle." There were other uncles, and I have no doubt they gave presents freely, for it was a wealthy and free-handed family ; but there was no other uncle who sent such a delicate and delightful reminder with every gift, to breathe a soft memory of him by day and by night.

.   .   .   .

I did my courting in the sweet atmosphere of that house, and, although I had no earthly desire to live in Boston, I could not help missing that strangely blended odor when my wife and I moved into an old house in an old

part of New York, whose former owners had
no connections in the Eastern trade. It was
a charming and home-like old house ; but at
first, although my wife had brought some be-
longings from her father's house, we missed
the pleasant flavor of our aromatic uncle, for
he was now my uncle, as well as my wife's.
I say at first, for we did not miss it long.
Uncle David—that was his name—not only
continued to send his fragrant gifts to my
wife at Christmas and upon her birthday, but
he actually adopted me, too, and sent me
Chinese cabinets and Chinese gods in various
minerals and metals, and many articles de-
signed for a smoker's use, which no smoker
would ever want to touch with a ten-foot
pole. But I cared very little about the
utility of these presents, for it was not many
years before, among them all, they set up
that exquisite perfume in the house, which
we had learned to associate with our aromatic uncle.

"Foo-choo-li, China, January—, 18—.

"Dear Nephew and Niece : The Present
is to inform you that I have this day shipped

to your address, per Steamer Ocean Queen, one marble and ebony Table, six assorted gods, and a blue Dinner set; also that I purpose leaving this Country for a visit to the Land of my Nativity on the 6th of March next, and will, if same is satisfactory to you, take up my Abode temporarily in your household. Should same not be satisfactory, please cable at my charge. Messrs. Smithson & Smithson, my Customs Brokers, will attend to all charges on the goods, and will deliver them at your readiness. The health of this place is better than customary by reason of the cool weather, which Health I am as usual enjoying. Trusting that you both are at present in the possession of the same Blessing, and will so continue, I remain, dear nephew and niece,

"Your affectionate

"UNCLE."

.   .   .   .

This was, I believe, by four dozen words—those which he used to inform us of his intention of visiting America—the longest letter that Uncle David had ever written to any member of his family. It also conveyed more

TOLD HIM ALL THE THINGS THAT I SHOULD NOT HAVE KNOWN
HOW TO SAY

information about himself than he had ever
given since the day he ran away to sea. Of
course we cabled the old gentleman that we
should be delighted to see him.

And, late that Spring, at some date at
which he could not possibly have been expected to arrive, he turned up at our house.

Of course we had talked a great deal about
him, and wondered what manner of a man we
should find him. Between us, my wife and I
had got an idea of his personal appearance
which I despair of conveying in words.
Vaguely, I should say that we had pictured
him as something mid-way between an ab-
normally tall Chinese mandarin and a bene-
volent Quaker. What we found when we got
home and were told that our uncle from
India was awaiting us, was a shrunken and
bent old gentleman, dressed very cleanly and
neatly in black broadcloth, with a limp,
many pleated shirt-front of old-fashioned
style, and a plain black cravat. If he had
worn an old-time stock we could have for-
given him the rest of the disappointment he
cost us; but we had to admit to ourselves
that he had the most absolutely commonplace
appearance of all our acquaintance. In fact,

we soon discovered that, except for a taciturnity the like of which we had never encountered, our aromatic uncle had positively not one picturesque characteristic about him. Even his aroma was a disappointment. He had it, but it was patchouly or some other cheap perfume of the sort, wherewith he scented his handkerchief, which was not even a bandanna, but a plain decent white one of the unnecessarily large sort which clergymen and old gentlemen affect.

But, even if we could not get one single romantic association to cluster about him, we very soon got to like the old gentleman. It is true that at our first meeting, after saying " How d'ye do " to me and receiving in impassive placidity the kiss which my wife gave him, he relapsed into dead silence, and continued to smoke a clay pipe with a long stem and a short bowl. This instrument he filled and re-filled every few minutes, and it seemed to be his only employment.) We plied him with questions, of course, but to these he responded with a wonderful brevity. In the course of an hour's conversation we got from him that he had had a pleasant voyage, that it was not a long voyage, that

it was not a short voyage, that it was about
the usual voyage, that he had not been sea-
sick, that he was glad to be back, and that
he was not surprised to find the country
very much changed. This last piece of information was repeated in the form of a
simple "No," given in reply to the direct
question; and although it was given politely,
and evidently without the least unamiable
intent, it made us both feel very cheap.
After all, it *was* absurd to ask a man if he
were surprised to find the country changed
after fifty or sixty years of absence. Unless
he was an idiot, and unable to read at that,
he must have expected something of the
sort.

But we grew to like him. He was
thoroughly kind and inoffensive in every
way. He was entirely willing to be talked
to, but he did not care to talk. If it was
absolutely necessary, he *could* talk, and when
he did talk he always made me think of the
" French-English Dictionary for the Pocket,"
compiled by the ingenious Mr. John Bellows;
for nobody except that extraordinary Eng-
lishman could condense a greater amount of
information into a smaller number of words.

During the time of his stay with us I think I learned more about China than any other man in the United States knew, and I do not believe that the aggregate of his utterances in the course of that six months could have amounted to one hour's continuous talk. Don't ask me for the information. I had no sort of use for it, and I forgot it as soon as I could. I like Chinese bric-à-brac, but my interest in China ends there.

Yet it was not long before Uncle David slid into his own place in the family circle. We soon found that he did not expect us to entertain him. He wanted only to sit quiet and smoke his pipe, to take his two daily walks by himself, and to read the daily paper one afternoon and Macaulay's "History of England" the next. He was never tired of sitting and gazing amiably but silently at my wife; and, to head the list of his good points, he would hold the baby by the hour, and for some mysterious reason that baby, who required the exhibition of seventeen toys in a minute to be reasonably quiet in the arms of anybody else, would sit placidly in Uncle David's lap, teething away steadily on the old gentleman's watch-chain, as quiet and as sol-

emu and as aged in appearance as any one of
the assorted gods of porcelain and jade and
ivory which our aromatic uncle had sent us.

.　　.　　.　　.　　.　　.　　.　　.

The old house in Boston was a thing of the
past. My wife's parents had been dead for
some years, and no one remained of her immediate family except a certain Aunt Lucretia, who had lived with them until shortly
before our marriage, when the breaking up of
the family sent her West to find a home with
a distant relative in California. We asked
Uncle Davy if he had stopped to see Aunt
Lucretia as he came through California. He
said he had not. We asked him if he wanted
to have Aunt Lucretia invited on to pass a
visit during his stay with us. He answered
that he did not. This did not surprise us at
all. You might think that a brother might
long to see a sister from whom he had been
separated nearly all of a long lifetime, but
then you might never have met Aunt Lucretia. My wife made the offer only from a
sense of duty ; and only after a contest with
me which lasted three days and nights.
Nothing but loss of sleep during an ex-

ceptionally busy time at my office induced
me to consent to her project of inviting
Aunt Lucretia. When Uncle David put
his veto upon the proposition I felt that
he might have taken back all his rare and
costly gifts, and I could still have loved
him.

But Aunt Lucretia came, all the same. My
wife is afflicted with a New England conscience, originally of a most uncomfortable
character. It has been much modified and
ameliorated, until it is now considerably less
like a case of moral hives ; but some wretched
lingering remnant of the original article induced her to write to Aunt Lucretia that
Uncle David was staying with us, and of
course Aunt Lucretia came without invitation
and without warning, dropping in on us with
ruthless unexpectedness.

.   .   .   .

You may not think, from what I have said,
that Aunt Lucretia's visit was a pleasant
event. But it was, in some respects ; for it
was not only the shortest visit she ever paid
us, but it was the last with which she ever
honored us.

She arrived one morning shortly after breakfast, just as we were preparing to go out for a drive. She would not have been Aunt Lucretia if she had not upset somebody's calculations at every turn of her existence. We welcomed her with as much hypocrisy as we could summon to our aid on short notice, and she was not more than usually offensive, although she certainly did herself full justice in telling us what she thought of us for not inviting her as soon as we even heard of Uncle David's intention to return to his native land. She said she ought to have been the first to embrace her beloved brother—to whom I don't believe she had given one thought in more years than I have yet seen.

Uncle David was dressing for his drive. His long residence in tropical countries had rendered him sensitive to the cold, and although it was a fine, clear September day, with the thermometer at about sixty, he was industriously building himself up with a series of overcoats. On a really snappy day I have known him to get into six of these garments; and when he entered the room on this occasion I think he had on five, at least.

My wife had heard his familiar foot on the stairs, and Aunt Lucretia had risen up and braced herself for an outburst of emotional affection.   I could see that it was going to be such a greeting as is given only once in two or three centuries, and then on the stage.   I felt sure it would end in a swoon, and I was looking around for a sofa-pillow for the old lady to fall upon, for from what I knew of Aunt Lucretia I did not believe she had ever swooned enough to be able to go through the performance without danger to her aged person.

But I need not have troubled myself.   Uncle David toddled into the room, gazed at Aunt Lucretia without a sign of recognition in his features, and toddled out into the hall, where he got his hat and gloves, and went out to the front lawn, where he always paced up and down for a few minutes before taking a drive, in order to stimulate his circulation.   This was a surprise, but Aunt Lucretia's behavior was a greater surprise. The moment she set eyes on Uncle David the theatrical fervor went out of her entire system, literally in one instant; and an absolutely natural, unaffected astonishment

displayed itself in her expressive and strong-
ly marked features. For almost a minute,
until the sound of Uncle David's footsteps
had died away, she stood absolutely rigid ;
while my wife and I gazed at her spell-
bound.

Then Aunt Lucretia pointed one long bony
finger at me, and hissed out with a true femi-
nine disregard of grammar :

"That aint *him !* "

.   .   .   .

"David," said Aunt Lucretia, impressively,
"had only one arm. He lost the other in
Madagascar."

I was too dumbfounded to take in the situation. I remember thinking, in a vague sort
of way, that Madagascar was a curious sort of
place to go for the purpose of losing an arm ;
but I did not apprehend the full significance
of this disclosure until I heard my wife's distressed protestations that Aunt Lucretia must
be mistaken ; there must be some horrible
mistake somewhere.

But Aunt Lucretia was not mistaken, and
there was no mistake anywhere. The arm
had been lost, and lost in Madagascar, and

14

she could give the date of the occurrence, and the circumstances attendant. Moreover, she produced her evidence on the spot. It was an old daguerreotype, taken in Calcutta a year or two after the Madagascar episode. She had it in her hand-bag, and she opened it with fingers trembling with rage and excitement. It showed two men standing side by side near one of those three-foot Ionic pillars that were an indispensable adjunct of photography in its early stages. One of the men was large, broad-shouldered, and handsome—unmistakably a handsome edition of Aunt Lucretia. His empty left sleeve was pinned across his breast. The other man was making allowance for the difference in years, no less unmistakably the Uncle David who was at that moment walking to and fro under our windows. For one instant my wife's face lighted up.

"Why, Aunt Lucretia," she cried, "there he is! That's Uncle David, dear Uncle David."

"There he is *not*," replied Aunt Lucretia. "That's his business partner—some common person that he picked up on the ship he first sailed in—and, upon my word, I do believe

"YOU'RE MY OWN DEAR UNCLE DAVID, ANYWAY!"

it's that wretched creature outside. And I'll Uncle David *him*."

She marched out like a grenadier going to battle, and we followed her meekly. There was, unfortunately, no room for doubt in the case. It only needed a glance to see that the man with one arm was a member of my wife's family, and that the man by his side, *our* Uncle David, bore no resemblance to him in stature or features.

Out on the lawn Aunt Lucretia sailed into the dear old gentleman in the five overcoats with a volley of vituperation. He did not interrupt her, but stood patiently to the end, listening, with his hands behind his back; and when, with her last gasp of available breath, Aunt Lucretia demanded:

"Who—who—who *are* you, you wretch?" he responded, calmly and respectfully:

"I'm Tommy Biggs, Miss Lucretia."

But just here my wife threw herself on his neck and hugged him, and cried:

"You're my own dear Uncle David, *anyway!*"

It was a fortunate, a gloriously fortunate, inspiration. Aunt Lucretia drew herself up in speechless scorn, stretched forth her bony finger, tried to say something and failed, and then she and her hand-bag went out of my gates, never to come in again.

.   .   .   .

When she had gone, our aromatic uncle—for we shall always continue to think of him in that light, or rather in that odor—looked thoughtfully after her till she disappeared, and then made one of the few remarks I ever knew him to volunteer.

"Ain't changed a mite in forty-seven years."

Up to this time I had been in a dazed condition of mind. As I have said, my wife's family was extinct save for herself and Aunt Lucretia, and she remembered so little of her parents, and she looked herself so little like Aunt Lucretia, that it was small wonder that neither of us remarked Uncle David's unlikeness to the family type. We knew that he did not resemble the ideal we had formed of him; and that had been the only consideration we had given to his looks. Now, it took only a moment of reflection to recall the fact that all the members of the family had been tall and shapely, and that even between the

ugly ones, like Aunt Lucretia, and the pretty
ones, like my wife, there was a certain resemblance. Perhaps it was only the nose—
the nose is the brand in most families, I believe—but whatever it was, I had only to see
my wife and Aunt Lucretia together to realize that the man who had passed himself off
as our Uncle David had not one feature in
common with either of them—nor with the
one-armed man in the daguerreotype. I was
thinking of this, and looking at my wife's
troubled face, when our aromatic uncle
touched me on the arm.

"I'll explain," he said, "to you. *You* tell
her."

We dismissed the carriage, went into the
house, and sat down. The old gentleman
was perfectly cool and collected, but he lit his
clay pipe, and reflected for a good five minutes before he opened his mouth. Then he
began:

"Finest man in the world, sir. Finest *boy*
in the world. Never anything like him.
But, peculiarities. Had 'em. Peculiarities.
Wouldn't write home. Wouldn't—" here he
hesitated—" send things home. I had to do
it. Did it for him. Didn't want his folks to

know. Other peculiarities. Never had any money. Other peculiarities. Drank. Other peculiarities. Ladies. Finest man in the world, all the same. Nobody like him. Kept him right with his folks for thirty-one years. Then died. Fever. Canton. Never been myself since. Kept right on writing, all the same. Also—" here he hesitated again— "sending things. Why? Don't know. Been a fool all my life. Never could do anything but make money. No family, no friends. Only *him*. Ran away to sea to look after him. Did look after him. Thought maybe your wife would be some like him. Barring peculiarities, she is. Getting old. Came here for company. Meant no harm. Didn't calculate on Miss Lucretia."

Here he paused and smoked reflectively for a minute or two.

"Hot in the collar — Miss Lucretia. Haughty. Like him, some. Just like she was forty-seven years ago. Slapped my face one day when I was delivering meat, because my jumper wasn't clean. Ain't changed a mite."

This was the first condensed statement of the case of our aromatic uncle. It was

THE DUPLICITY OF WHICH HE HAD BEEN GUILTY WEIGHED
ON HIS SPIRIT

only in reply to patient, and, I hope, loving, gentle, and considerate questioning that the whole story came out—at once pitiful and noble—of the poor little butcher-boy who ran away to sea to be body-guard, servant, and friend to the splendid, showy, selfish youth whom he worshipped; whose heartlessness he cloaked for many a long year, who lived upon his bounty, and who died in his arms, nursed with a tenderness surpassing that of a brother. And as far as I could find out, ingratitude and contempt had been his only reward.

.   .   .   .

I need not tell you that when I repeated all this to my wife she ran to the old gentleman's room and told him all the things that I should not have known how to say— that we cared for him; that we wanted him to stay with us; that he was far, far more our uncle than the brilliant, unprincipled scapegrace who had died years before, dead for almost a lifetime to the family who idolized him; and that we wanted him to stay with us as long as kind heaven would let him. But it was of no use. A change had come over our aromatic uncle which we could both of us see, but could not understand. The duplicity of which he had been guilty weighed on his spirit. The next day he went out for his usual walk, and he never came back. We used every means of search and inquiry, but we never heard from him until we got this letter from Foo-choo-li :

.   .   .   .

" DEAR NEPHEW AND NIECE : The present is to inform you that I am enjoying the Health that might be expected at my Age, and in my condition of Body, which is to say bad. I ship you by to-day's steamer, Pacific Monarch, four dozen jars of ginger, and two dozen ditto preserved oranges, to which I would have added some other Comfits, which I purposed offering for your acceptance, if it were not that my Physician has forbidden me to leave my Bed. In case of Fatal Results from this trying Condition, my Will, duly attested, and made in your favor, will be placed in your hands by Messrs. Smithson & Smithson, my Customs Brokers, who will also pay all charges on goods sent. The Health of this place being unfavorably af-

fected by the Weather, you are unlikely to
hear more from,

      "Dear Nephew and Niece,

           "Your affectionate

                "Uncle."

And we never did hear more—except for
his will—from Our Aromatic Uncle; but our
whole house still smells of his love.

Exit Our Aromatic Uncle